## Books by Tom Hoffman

Bartholomew the Adventurer • The Eleventh Ring
Bartholomew the Adventurer • The Thirteenth Monk
Bartholomew the Adventurer • The Seventh Medallion

•••

Orville Mouse and the Puzzle of the Clockwork Glowbirds
Orville Mouse and the Puzzle of the Shattered Abacus
Orville Mouse and the Puzzle of the Capricious Shadows
Orville Mouse and the Puzzle of the Last Metaphonium
Orville Mouse and the Puzzle of the Sagacious Sapling

•••

The Translucent Boy and the Girl Who Saw Him
The Translucent Boy and the Cat Who Ran Out of Time
The Translucent Boy and the Girl Who Dreamed She Could Fly
The Translucent Boy and the Man Who Walked to the Moon
The Translucent Boy and the Children of Ice

•••

The Comet Kid Chronicles • Under the Blue Comet
The Comet Kid Chronicles • The Unfocused Man
The Comet Kid Chronicles • The Sinister Sorcerer

•••

The Ghost Ring • Welcome to Wilder House
The Ghost Ring • Shadows of Caligo Falls

# THE GHOST RING

## SHADOWS OF CALIGO FALLS

# TOM HOFFMAN

Cover design by Tom Hoffman Graphic Design
Anchorage, Alaska

Tom Hoffman
Visit my website at thoffmanak.wordpress.com
Email: OrvilleMouse@gmail.com

Printed in the United States of America

First Printing: 2024
ISBN 979-8-9884059-3-1

**For Tom Beauvais**

Santa is real and
he lives in Alaska.

**"In one drop of water are found all the secrets of the oceans."**

*Kahlil Gibran*

"The cave you fear to enter
holds the treasure you seek."

*Joseph Campbell*

# THE GHOST RING

## RING

### SHADOWS OF CALIGO FALLS

# Chapter 1

Simon Moody shivered, pulling the covers up to his chin, his eyes darting around the room. It was the middle of July, the early morning sun streaming in through his bedroom window, but the icy chill in the air belonged to a frosty morning in December.

This was not the first unnatural ghostly chill Simon had experienced. When he and his mom first arrived in Caligo Falls, Marion Jaggers, the estate attorney, had given them a brief tour of Wilder House, the immense Victorian mansion they had inherited from Simon's great uncle, Edmund Wilder. The eerie chill had rolled through Simon when Marion stopped on the grand staircase landing to point out a collection of extremely valuable oil paintings adorning the wall.

Kate Moody hadn't felt the chill, but Simon had, and

later his new best friend Clara Barley felt it, confessing to him that she believed in the existence of ghosts, and could sense their presence.

Of course he had no way of knowing it at the time, but when they stopped on the landing, Simon had been standing next to the ghost of Edward Briggs, one of the more unfortunate spectral beings inhabiting Wilder House long after his untimely demise.

There had been other restless spirits residing in Wilder House, but most had moved on to the next realm, thanks to Simon and Clara and the ancient bejeweled ring bequeathed to him by Edmund Wilder, the enigmatic and immensely wealthy artist. Simon would later learn the mysterious ring had originally been called the Sacred Shadow Ring of Persephone, but for simplicity's sake, Simon called it the ghost ring.

He eyed the golden bronze ring sitting on his bedside table, with its indecipherable symbols and sparkling green hexagonal stone. He had two choices: he could put the ghost ring on and discover the source of the unearthly chill, possibly a terrifying spectral phantasm staring at him with dark malevolence, or he could leave the ring where it lay.

"Sorry ghost, I've got places to go and things to do."

He hopped out of bed and pulled on his clothes, heading for the door, stopping abruptly to grab the ghost ring from the bedside table and slip it into his pocket. He gave a friendly wave to whatever chilling apparition might be occupying his bedroom. "Hey, ghost, I'm off to see my best friend Clara. You should take a stroll outside, catch a few rays while I'm gone. You're looking a little pale."

Simon laughed at his own joke as he stepped through the doorway into the lavishly furnished second floor sitting area, the wall closest to him lined with floor-to-ceiling mahogany bookshelves displaying a myriad of dusty leather bound volumes. He eyed the large bay window with its plush maroon velvet window seat, a seat occupied for many years by the ghost of beautiful Emma Weatherby as she waited patiently for Edmund Wilder to pass. His great uncle Edmund had known full well the power of the ghost ring, having used it to speak with his beloved Emma, Clara's grandmother, for many years. During his time with the ring, Edmund had helped innumerable other lost spirits find their way home, moving on to the next realm.

Edmund and his beloved Emma were gone now, but not before Emma had spoken at great length to Clara, pleading with her not to make the same choices she had made in her lifetime.

Simon loved the sitting area, with its intricate hand-woven carpets strategically placed beneath delicately embroidered stuffed armchairs, each with its own reading table and exquisite stained glass reading lamp. Three tall glass display cases sat against the far wall, replete with hundreds of curious antiquities collected by Edmund and his father.

Simon strolled down the magnificent curving grand staircase, stopping short when he heard his mom's voice echoing through the atrium. "Simon, Mrs. Morley has breakfast ready! She says it's getting cold! Hurry!"

Simon gave a silent groan. On the one hand, he had promised to pick up Clara in half an hour, but on the other hand, the very last thing he wanted to do was get on the wrong side of Mrs. Morley, quite possibly the most punctual individual he had ever encountered.

Mrs. Morley had been Edmund's cook for many years, his final will and testament stipulating that both Mrs. Morley and Harrington, the enigmatic Wilder House gardener, should remain employed at Wilder House for as long as they so desired.

It was only recently that Harrington's true identity had been revealed to Simon and Clara as Claudius, an Elder Guardian of the Six Rings of Persephone, having been sent to Caligo Falls from a secret temple hidden beneath the Temple of Demeter in Eleusis, Greece. The purpose of Harrington's presence in Wilder House was to watch over the Sacred Shadow Ring of Persephone after it had been stolen by a neophyte guardian named Asterius and sold to

Edmund Wilder in 1961.

"Simon! Breakfast!"

"Coming!" Simon raced down the stairs, passing through a series of long hallways and rooms. He finally reached the dining room, eyeing the twelve empty chairs lining each side of the thirty-foot-long gleaming mahogany table. "They must be in the kitchen."

He hurried down another long hallway, stopping at a plain white door, the austere entrance to the back hall of the house, once the domain of several dozen household servants. He pushed the door open, stepping into the kitchen, spotting his mom, Kate Moody, sitting at the simple rectangular kitchen table. Mrs. Morley stood at the stove, her back to Simon. She was a somewhat rotund woman wearing a crisp gray dress with a white collar, her gray hair coiled up in a tight bun.

"Good morning, Mrs. Morley. Breakfast smells great. Are those blueberry pancakes?"

"Better late than never. Yes, blueberry pancakes, your favorite. Take a seat, they're getting cold."

A smile crossed Kate's face. "Are you in a hurry to get somewhere? Off to meet someone?"

Mrs. Morley gave a snort. "Can't imagine who."

Simon said, "If you must know, I'm picking up Clara. We're going to the general store to get a few things."

"What kind of things?"

"Just some stuff we wanted to get."

"What kind of stuff?"

Simon looked up from his pancakes. "We're getting two LED flashlights, a little shovel, a metal detector, and some rope."

Mrs. Morley turned her head slightly, her ears perking up.

Kate gave Simon a puzzled look. "Why on earth do you need a metal detector?"

"Marion Jaggers said there's a secret tunnel behind one of the basement closets that leads to a hidden room. We're going to explore the tunnel, see what's in the secret room."

"Simon, that doesn't sound very safe at all. This house is old, built in 1905, suppose the tunnel collapses? I don't think that's a very wise thing to do, go poking around in an old tunnel."

"We'll be careful, I promise. Edmund told Marion about the tunnel and the secret room. We'll probably find cool old stuff there. That's why we have the metal detector. If it doesn't look safe we won't go in, I promise."

Simon had conveniently neglected to mention that Edmund had also said there was a skeleton in the secret room, possibly the earthly remains of someone murdered by his grandfather, and even more interesting, the tunnel was supposed to be haunted. Simon and Clara were drawn

8

TOM HOFFMAN

to the haunted tunnel like moths to a flame, the two friends being self-proclaimed paranormal investigators.

Twenty minutes later, after surreptitiously glancing at his watch more than a few times, Simon set down his fork. "Breakfast was wonderful, Mrs. Morley. The pancakes were delicious, but I should probably get going. I don't want to be late picking up Clara."

Mrs. Morley gave a knowing smile. "Give my regards to Clara. She's a lovely young lady, just about the age my dear Darlene was when she passed."

Simon nodded empathetically. He and Clara had never told Mrs. Morley, and they never would, that they had encountered Darlene's spirit at the lake near Wilder House where she had accidentally drowned in 1977. Darlene's spirit had been lost in a timeless dreamlike fog, but with help from the ghost of Robert Walker, a doctor dealing with severe anger issues after being murdered by his wife Bertha, Darlene had awakened, and was able to move on, eventually being reunited with her lost love, Ezra Durdles.

Kate pushed her chair back, standing up. "I'll help you with the dishes, Mrs. Morley."

"No need for that, I like to keep busy."

Simon headed for the back door. "I won't be long, I'm just going to the general store."

"Drive carefully."

"I will."

He hurried through the huge well-stocked pantry, eye-ing the shadowy stairway that led down to the basement of Wilder House, exiting through the back door, and mak-ing his way down the hill to the old carriage house.

Once used for horse drawn carriages, the lengthy two-story building now served as a five-car garage, currently holding four of Edmund Wilder's extremely valuable an-tique cars.

Simon's vehicle of choice, however, was a battered old green pickup truck from the 1950s, a truck which had once belonged to Edward Briggs, the previous caretaker of Wilder House, and the terrifying spirit who had occu-pied the landing on the grand staircase, the source of Si-mon's initial eerie chill.

Simon had wisely decided that driving around in a gleaming 1932 eight-cylinder Duesenberg worth over a million dollars would have been off-putting to the resi-dents of rural Caligo Falls, the old pickup truck being a far more appropriate choice.

He swung open the first garage door, stepping inside, flicking on the lights, eyeing the row of sparkling vintage cars. He liked the 1921 Stutz Bearcat, an amazing sports car in its day, but still preferred the battered old pickup, coincidentally well aware that Clara was not impressed in the least by ostentatious displays of great wealth.

Five minutes later his truck was rattling down the long winding gravel driveway that led to the main road, a narrow two-lane highway, the Caligo Falls town center a fifteen minute drive away.

He slowed down when he spotted the four-way stop ahead of him, deciding to say hello to Jeremiah Davis, see how his day was going.

Simon pulled over at the crossroads, removing the ghost ring from his pocket, slipping it onto his finger. It didn't take long for Jeremiah to appear, dressed in his dark suit and tie, riding his old-fashioned high-wheel bicycle, known back in the day as a Penny Farthing. The front wheel of the bike stood well over four feet tall, Jeremiah perched precariously on the seat above it, gripping the handle bars. The rear wheel was small, about eighteen inches. The bicycle looked extremely hard to ride, not to mention exceedingly hazardous to the rider's health.

"And there he is, right on time." Simon waited until Jeremiah was about fifteen feet from the crossroads, then pointed one finger at the tall spruce trees lining the road, saying, "Hello, huge moose."

At that very moment, a massive bull moose emerged from the dense forest, almost colliding with a startled Jeremiah Davis. Jeremiah swerved wildly, losing control of the Penny Farthing, tumbling over, falling, his head colliding sharply with a large granite boulder. He lay still,

11

blood running down the side of the rock. Fifteen seconds later, the enormous bull moose, Jeremiah, and his ancient Penny Farthing were gone, faded away to nothingness.

Jeremiah was the first ghost Simon had ever seen, although technically he wasn't a ghost as most people think of them. Edmund Wilder had studied ghosts for many years, describing, in notes found by Simon, three distinct varieties.

The first he called *ripples*, ghosts like Jeremiah, being the result of a single traumatic event that rippled across time. Every time Simon stopped at the crossroads, if he was wearing the ghost ring, he could watch as Jeremiah met his untimely end, but the reality was that Jeremiah had died only once, back in the summer of 1887, the tragic event rippling across time.

The second category of ghosts mentioned by Edmund were those who were fully conscious and aware of their surroundings, knowing they were no longer inhabitants of the physical world. Simon and Clara had met a few of those, including the angry ghost of Robert Sawyer, MD, who took great pleasure in tormenting his wife Bertha, payback for murdering him with a poison called aconitine.

Edmund called the last group *sleepers*, ghosts who were scarcely aware of their surroundings, drifting in a timeless haze, not realizing they were dead, mindlessly sleepwalking through the shadow world, the place between this world and the next. Mrs. Morley's daughter Darlene had been a sleeper, drifting around Ghost Lake, not knowing who or where she was.

Simon gave a long sigh, wondering why he felt compelled to watch Jeremiah meet his tragic end every time he stopped at the crossroads. It was a dreadful sight, but part of him thought it might bring some comfort to Jeremiah, wherever he was, to know that someone was remembering him, that he was not forgotten, that someone was remembering the very bad day he had in 1887.

Simon grabbed his phone when it beeped, reading a text from Clara.

*Where are you?*

*Almost there. Mrs. Morley made blueberry pancakes. I couldn't get away.*

Simon sped down the road toward the town center, turning right on Pine Street, pulling into the parking lot of the Caligo Falls Grocery Store. This was where he had first met Clara, the granddaughter of Emma Weatherby, the only woman Edmund Wilder had ever truly loved. His first meeting with Clara had been a disastrous one, Simon believing her to be the ghost of Emma Weatherby, Edmund's portraits of her bearing an astonishing resemblance to Clara. Needless to say, their initial meeting had not gone well. Simon had said it was something they would laugh about in twenty years, but it only took Clara a few weeks to laugh about it, describing in great detail the look on Simon's face when he first saw her.

Clara stepped out of the store, waving to him. Simon grinned when he saw her, waving back.

She ran over to the truck and hopped in. "I told Mr. Fernald I'd be gone for an hour or two, so we can't be longer than that."

"We'll have plenty of time." Simon put the truck in gear, pulling out of the parking lot onto Pine Street, driving until he saw the large green hand painted sign reading *Caligo Falls General Store*.

"Clever name, I wonder who thought that one up?"

"It is clever, but is it as clever as *Caligo Falls Grocery Store*?"

Simon laughed. "We're a long way from Brooklyn, that's for sure."

Clara studied his face. "You're still not sorry you moved here from New York?"

Simon took her hand. "I'm not. It was the best thing that ever happened to me, I just didn't know it at the time."

"Good answer. And, that's usually how life works, by the way."

They climbed out of the truck, walking across the hard packed dirt parking lot, entering into the dimly lit general store.

# Chapter 2

Clara called out, "Hi, Bobby!"

An older man with a receding hairline, round silver rimmed glasses, and a well-worn white canvas apron stepped out from behind the counter. "Hi, Clara. Hi, Simon. What are you guys up to today?"

"We just need to get a few things."

Simon glanced across the store to the rickety wooden staircase that led up to Marion Jagger's cluttered law office. He had asked Marion, a quirky but entirely formidable attorney, why she had a small cluttered office above a general store in the little town of Caligo Falls instead of a suite of offices in Manhattan. Simon knew she was very successful, and more than likely extremely wealthy. She told him it was for the same reason that Simon drove the battered old pickup truck instead of the flashy million dollar Duesenberg.

"Is Marion here today?"

"Not here, she left early this morning, all gussied up in a fancy suit, took the morning train to Manhattan.

Some big real estate deal going on, something about a skyscraper. She said everyone is suing everyone, there's probably going to be a few fist fights and a murder before it's all over."

Simon laughed. "That sounds like her."

"What can I help you find?"

"We need two LED flashlights, a small shovel, some nylon rope, and a metal detector."

"Going treasure hunting in a cave?"

Simon laughed. "Something like that."

Bobby shrugged. "I won't ask. We have everything here except the metal detector."

Clara said, "Does anyone else have them here in town?"

"I don't think so, but as luck would have it, I happen to have one in my truck you can borrow. How long do you need it for? I was going to use it this weekend, hunting for old relics."

"Just a day or two at the most."

"Not a problem then. Just drop it off here when you're done."

As they were strolling around the store Simon asked, "How long has the store been around? It looks really old."

"It is old. My great grandfather opened the doors in 1885. It's been in our family ever since."

Simon did the math. "So that means your grandfather would have been here around the same time as Edmund Wilder's grandfather?"

"He was a lot younger than Cornelius Wilder, but he was around then. Don't take this the wrong way, but I have heard that a lot of people weren't very fond of Cornelius Wilder."

Simon nodded. "I've heard that too. Harrington told us a little about him, and he used words like cruel and ruthless, saying Cornelius treated Edmund very badly when he was growing up."

"Sounds about right. My dad always said he was surprised by how nice Edmund was, coming from a family like that. His great grandfather was some kind of railroad tycoon back in the day, wasn't he? That's where all the money came from?"

"He was. Harrington said he was a hard man who cared for nothing but power and wealth."

"I guess it makes sense then, that Cornelius would be like him. The apple doesn't fall far from the tree."

Clara said, "It's sad when people are like that, missing out on the best things in life."

Bobby shrugged. "It's ancient history, probably best forgotten."

Simon grabbed two flashlights, dropping them into the basket. "That's it, we have everything."

"I'll put it on your tab. The metal detector is in the back of the red truck out front."

"Thanks, we really appreciate it, Bobby. We'll have it back in a day or two."

With the metal detector in hand, Simon and Clara headed back to the grocery store. As they were driving, Simon glanced over at Clara, noting her somber expression.

"What's the matter? Did we forget something?"

"I wasn't going to say anything, but you should probably know that Bobby's grandfather didn't have a happy life. That's what my mom told me."

"What happened to him?"

"He was an alcoholic, she said he took his own life."

Simon frowned. "That's not good. Now I feel bad for asking about him. I just thought he might have known Cornelius Wilder."

"He probably knew of him, but they lived in very different worlds."

"Good point, the haves and the have-nots." Simon turned into the grocery store, parking by the front door. Clara leaned over, giving him a quick hug. "Don't forget, tomorrow is skeleton hunting day at Wilder House."

"I think I'd rather see a ghost than a skeleton."

"It can't be any worse than when Asterius had you dig up his body down by the pump house."

Simon grimaced. "That was bad. I had to put that sacred jeweled dagger in his hand."

"So he could enter the Elysian Fields."

"I hope it worked."

"Cheer up, think how much fun we'll have hunting for clues in the tunnel. This will be the first official case for Barley & Moody Paranormal Investigations."

"I thought we decided call it Moody & Barley. Wait, who's paying us?"

"We decided to list our names alphabetically so it would be completely unbiased, no favoritism, so Barley & Moody it is. And no one is paying us, it's a pro bono case."

Simon laughed. "I don't recall deciding to put our names in alphabetical order, but I'll let it go for now. I'm going to head back home and search through Edmund's trove of old newspaper articles and journals for any information about Cornelius and the secret tunnel. Maybe I'll find an obituary for whoever got murdered in the secret room."

"Text me if you find something."

"I will."

Simon drove down the highway toward Wilder House, coming to a stop at the crossroads, calling out, "Hey, Jeremiah, have a great day! Watch out for that moose!"

He parked the truck in the carriage house, grabbing their purchases from the general store, grinning. Clara was right, it was going to be fun looking for clues together.

The icy chill hit him when he was halfway up the hill. He stopped, glancing around. This was the first time he had felt the eerie chill outside of Wilder House. A curious thought popped into his head, the words he had spoken to the entity that morning coming back to him. *You should take a stroll outside, catch a few rays while I'm gone. You're looking a little pale.*

Maybe the ghost had taken his suggestion to heart. Was that even possible? If it was true, the ghost might not be as scary as he had imagined.

"Okay, potentially friendly ghost, let's see who you are." Simon set down the packages, reaching into his pocket for the ghost ring. The chill was getting stronger, he was shivering. Unfortunately, or possibly fortunately, the moment Simon slipped on the ring was the moment the chill vanished. He looked around, seeing nothing, not a single ghost in sight, friendly or otherwise.

He called out, "Just so you know, you might be a friendly ghost, but you're getting a little annoying."

He entered the house through the servants' entrance, stepping into the pantry, walking down the shadowy wooden stairs to the basement.

21

He was not fond of the basement storage area, with its musty clutter and the long row of creepy closets. Taking a deep breath he pushed the button on the antiquated wall switch, a single incandescent bulb dangling from the basement ceiling blinking on.

He was remembering the first time he had seen this section of the basement. It looked like a set torn from a horror movie, piles of dusty old furniture, boxes, dozens of lamps, bed frames, stacks of old metal steamer trunks covered with travel stickers, innumerable picture frames scattered across the room, sets of old golf clubs, and the row of seven closet doors lining the left wall.

"Those doors are so creepy. I don't even want to know what's in there. I wish Clara was here, she'd say something funny."

He eyed the row of pale blue doors, the paint chipped and peeling. They would have to move a lot of furniture before they could open the doors.

He pressed on, making his way across the basement through the maze of antique furniture, brushing aside the cobwebs, reaching the plain wooden door that opened to the old servants' quarters.

Stepping through into a long hallway lined with plain white doors, he pushed the light switch, a row of overhead light bulbs clicking on, one of them flickering. A good number of the household servants had lived down here, each of their small rooms holding a wooden cot, dresser, wardrobe and a wash basin.

Simon stopped at the fourth door, remembering it was the room that held the old photograph. He pushed the door open, looking in. The photograph was still on the dresser, a dusty wooden picture frame with cracked glass holding a sepia tone image of a young boy, a small carved wooden horse in his hand. The boy was not smiling, and his clothes were well worn. Simon studied his face. Would he know Simon was remembering him, looking at his photo? A curious wave of sadness rolled through Simon. He had no idea why the photograph affected him this way.

He closed the door, heading down the hall, arriving at a tall ornately paneled door with a hand carved oaken frame, a polished ornamental brass transom above it. This was the elaborate entrance to the front hall of the house, the area of Wilder House reserved solely for family members and their esteemed guests.

He entered a spacious, elegant room, three exquisite crystal chandeliers hanging from the ceiling. An antique oaken roll top desk sat against the left wall, comfortable armchairs and embroidered sofas resting on a plush midnight blue carpet, bookshelves lining the right wall. This was one of Edmund's private studies, a refuge when he sought a quiet retreat from the world.

Simon strode over to a heavy steel door, looking re-markably out of place in a lavishly appointed Victorian study. He ran his hand across its rows of metal rivets. "Incongruous, that's the word I would use." He leaned over, pulling up a corner of the plush carpet, retrieving a heavy brass key. He inserted the key into a silver panel next to the door and turned it, rewarded by the whining sound of a powerful electric motor, the vault room door sliding open.

Simon entered the vault room, once solely the private domain of Edmund Wilder. The steel door slid shut when he clicked on the overhead lights.

The vault room was actually two rooms. The first one was a functional but quite ordinary looking office. Shelves on the closest wall were lined with dozens of leather bound journals recounting Edmund's numerous and varied travels abroad, including his remarkable ex-periences at the Temple of Demeter in Eleusis, Greece, where he had purchased the ghost ring from Asterius, the neophyte Guardian of the Sacred Rings who had stolen it.

There were also long rows of account ledgers, listing every artifact purchased by Edmund and his father, not-ing in detail where and when the object had been pur-chased, and the price paid for it. Along the opposite wall stood a row of four wooden cabinets with three-foot-wide shallow drawers and small gleaming brass handles, the drawers holding hundreds of Edmund's sketches: pencil drawings, charcoal renderings, and watercolor sketches, all used as reference material for his finished oil paintings.

Simon turned to face two six-foot-tall wooden cabinets, each with eight drawers, the drawers lined with purple velvet and filled with many hundreds of ancient gold coins, and impossibly valuable pieces of antique jewelry. Each item bore a numbered tag, referencing it to the appropriate account ledger.

Simon pulled open one of the drawers, studying the gold coins, picking one up. The inscription was in Latin, so it was probably from ancient Rome, but the identity of the emperor whose portrait was imprinted on the coin was a mystery. He set the coin back down, closing the drawer. He and his mom had decided that one day they would donate the contents of the two wooden cabinets to a museum.

Simon walked across the room to an intricately carved wooden panel covered with curious symbols. Kate had discovered it, the secret door leading up the stairs to the second room, Edmund's art studio.

He pushed the panel open, walking up the steps, entering into a spacious room with twenty-foot high ceilings, the studio illuminated by sunlight flooding in through a dozen vertical windows on the far wall.

This was where Edmund created most of his oil paintings, the studio holding several large oaken easels, tables covered with tubes of oil paint, jars of solvent and linseed oil, and hundreds of brushes resting in ceramic vases and wooden boxes. Many dozens of finished oil paintings were stored in long wooden racks against the back wall.

He stepped over to a round hardwood table covered with stacks of black binders, each binder holding hundreds of old newspaper clippings collected by Edmund and his father. Many of the clippings were obituaries, including one for the bicycle rider Jeremiah Davis, killed in 1887. Jeremiah was coincidentally also the first ghost Edmund Wilder had seen using the ghost ring. Along with the obituaries were numerous articles about people Edmund and his father had known from their travels abroad. Simon flipped open one of the binders.

"Let's see what we can find out about old Cornelius Wilder."

# Chapter 3

After almost an hour of sifting through stacks of yellowed newspaper clippings, Simon's eyelids were drooping. He had recognized a few names in the obituaries, but not many. Harrington once told him that Edmund had aided hundreds of lost spirits over the years, helping them to move on, but Simon had no idea who they had been. One binder was filled with obituaries from eight or nine different countries, Simon recognizing only a few of the languages.

He continued his search, finally hitting pay dirt when he spotted Cornelius Wilder's name in an old yellowed newspaper clipping. The article contained a photograph of two men standing in front of a luxurious old fashioned touring car, but it wasn't one of the antique cars currently residing in the carriage house.

The article was brief, pulled from the society page of the New York Tribune in January of 1917.

*Railroad tycoon Cornelius Wilder has made his triumphant return to Manhattan from Greenville, shown here accompanied by his new bodyguard and personal chauffeur, Mr. Tobias Granger. The two men posed for a photograph in front of Mr. Wilder's recent acquisition, a top-of-the-line luxurious 1917 Rolls Royce Silver Ghost.*

Simon studied the photo, noting that both men were smiling, not what he expected to see after everything he had been told about Cornelius. He set the article aside, moving on, sorting through Edmund's seemingly endless collection of newspaper clippings and photographs.

He found a number of interesting articles, including one from 1918 recording the first documented case of the deadly Spanish Flu in Caligo Falls. Simon had learned about the 1918 pandemic in history class, how a deadly new strain of the influenza virus had caused over six hundred thousand deaths in the United States alone. It was a terrifying time, many people dying only a day or two after being infected by the virus.

He was methodically making his way through the third binder when he found a photograph of two men shaking hands in a hospital room, instantly recognizing them as Cornelius Wilder and his bodyguard, Tobias Granger, the same two men he had seen standing in front of the 1917 Rolls Royce Silver Ghost. This article was dated July 19, 1916, written before the society page article had appeared in the Tribune.

## *Heroic Act Saves Railroad Tycoon's Life*

*In a startling turn of events yesterday, a remarkable act of bravery by Tobias Granger, a foreman with the Midland & Southern Railways, saved the life of Mr. Cornelius Wilder, the railway's highly esteemed owner. The dramatic incident unfolded at the Greenville Train Depot, where Mr. Wilder was addressing a large gathering of reporters and railroad employees there to inaugurate the new M&S Greenville to Chicago line.*

*Without warning, an armed assailant emerged from the crowd, intent on causing grievous harm to Mr. Wilder. With commendable valor, Mr. Granger stepped forth, positioning himself between the attacker and Mr. Wilder. In the ensuing struggle, a single shot was discharged, striking Mr. Granger in the leg.*

*Thanks to Mr. Granger's courageous intervention, Mr. Wilder emerged from the incident unscathed. Nearby officers swiftly subdued the attacker, preventing any further violence. Mr. Granger received immediate medical attention and is currently recuperating from his injury.*

*In a heartfelt gesture of gratitude, Mr. Wilder has extended an offer to Mr. Granger to serve as his personal chauffeur and bodyguard. "Mr. Granger's heroism has highlighted the bravery and selflessness present within our community," stated Mr. Wilder in an official announcement. "I am honored to employ such a man as Mr. Granger, a true hero in every sense of the word."*

*The Greenville Gazette commends Mr. Granger for his bravery and wishes him a swift recovery.*

Simon rubbed his eyes, stretching. "At least he rewarded the guy for saving his life, that's something. I'm starving." He glanced at his watch, sitting up straight. "Almost time for dinner, I can't be late. I'll ask Harrington if he knows anything about the chauffeur who saved Cornelius' life. It could be a clue."

He grabbed the two newspaper clippings and exited the studio, passing through the music room, exercise room, and a small library, emerging at the base of the wide marble staircase leading up to the first floor. He raced up the stairs to the two-story foyer just in time to catch his mom coming down the grand staircase.

"Am I late for dinner?"

Kate shook her head. "Right on time. Oh, Harrington is back from Deep River. He'll be joining us."

"Nice, I need to ask him something about Cornelius Wilder."

"Did you find that secret tunnel you were looking for?"

"Not yet, Clara's coming by tomorrow to help me look for it. We have to move a lot of old furniture."

They strolled into the main dining room, Harrington already seated at the imposing mahogany table. He stood up when they entered the room, stepping over and pulling out a chair out for Kate.

"Honestly, Harrington, you really don't need to do that."

"Old habits die hard, I'm afraid."

Simon took a seat, setting the newspaper clippings on the table.

Harrington glanced at them, then said, "I see you have been perusing Edmund's rather extensive collection of old newspaper clippings."

Simon laughed. "The key word there is extensive. I'm trying to find out more about his grandfather, Cornelius Wilder. I've only found two articles about him. The first one was about Tobias Granger, a foreman who saved Cornelius' life in 1916 when some guy tried to shoot him. It said that Cornelius hired Tobias to be his chauffeur and bodyguard, his way of thanking him. The other article is a picture of Cornelius and Tobias Granger standing next to a big luxury Rolls Royce in Manhattan in 1917." Simon slid the clippings across the table to Harrington.

Harrington studied the images. "That is most certainly Cornelius Wilder, but I am not familiar with the chauffeur. This was long before my time, of course. I do recall Edmund mentioning his grandfather had a number of bodyguards over the years, but that is the extent of my knowledge."

"Why did he need bodyguards?"

"Apparently there were a great many people who were not fond of him, many holding him solely responsible for the loss of their property and homes. During the westward expansion of the railroads, a great deal of land, including established family farms, was seized by the railroads."

"How could they just take their land?"

"The railroads had been granted the power of eminent domain, allowing them to seize whatever lands necessary to build their new tracks. The expansion of the railroad lines was deemed vital to the growth of the country."

"That doesn't seem fair."

Kate said, "They still do that today. If the government needs to reroute a big highway, they can use eminent domain to take your land, but they have to pay you for it, whatever the current value is."

Mrs. Morley stepped into the room, wearing her signature crisp gray dress and white collar. "Dinner will be served in five minutes."

32

"Thank you, Mrs. Morley. Everything smells delicious."

Simon turned when he heard a sharp rapping on the front door. "Who's that?"

"Are you expecting anyone? Clara?"

"No. I'll go see who it is." He jumped up and ran to the foyer, peering through the window. Marion Jaggers was standing on the porch, motioning for him to open the door.

Marion stepped inside before Simon could invite her in. She sniffed the air. "Smells good, what are you having for dinner?"

"I'm not sure. Maybe stew?"

"Perfect, I'll join you. I just got back from New York. I have something for you. We can eat first. Is it beef stew?"

"I don't know. You brought something from New York? What is it?"

"Top secret. I don't even know what it is."

Marion headed into the main dining room, Simon trailing behind her.

"Greetings all, sorry to barge in on you like this. Important business for Mr. Simon Moody, resident of Wilder House."

Kate gave her a questioning look. "What kind of business?"

"The Edmund Wilder kind. He wanted Simon to have something exactly three months after you became legal owners of the Wilder estate."

Simon glanced at his mom, then back at Marion. The first mysterious gift Edmund had left for him was the ghost ring, and along with it came a cryptic note, a quote from Shakespeare's *Hamlet*.

*There are more things in heaven and earth, Horatio, than are dreamt of in your philosophy.*

The note's meaning had become very clear to Simon once he realized the ring allowed him to see and communicate with ghosts.

"You don't know what he left me?"

Marion pulled a six-inch-long box from her pocket, carefully wrapped in brown paper, securely tied with coarse green twine. "No idea what's in it. A big old mystery wrapped in an enigma, just like Edmund. I'm famished. We can open it after dinner. Big real estate deal today in Manhattan, we should crack open a bottle of champagne, celebrate. Where's Clara? I thought you two were lovebirds, never apart." She snorted, slapping the table.

Simon studiously adjusted the silverware next to his plate. "She's doing something with her mom tonight."

34

Harrington was eyeing the box curiously.

Mrs. Morley stepped into the dining room, carrying a large silver platter, stopping short when she saw Marion Jaggers seated at the table. She did not look pleased.

Kate looked up, saying, "I'm so sorry, Mrs. Morley, we had a surprise visit from Marion. She has something she needs to discuss with us. Would it be all right if she joined us for dinner? She's had a long train ride from New York."

"Of course, madam. I shall prepare another setting." She set the tray down on the table, her laser sharp eyes on Marion. She turned and left the room.

Marion grinned. "My bad, I hope she doesn't poison my food."

Harrington said, "Mrs. Morley likes everything to run smoothly, according to plan. She was not always like this, but after Darlene disappeared she became rather averse to unexpected events."

Marion's grin vanished. "Noted and acknowledged."

Dinner proved to be delicious, Marion mending her fences with Mrs. Morley, complimenting her cooking and promising her a lovely bottle of French wine to make up for her unannounced appearance.

Mrs. Morley was smiling by the time she brought out dessert, a beautifully decorated chocolate cake. She set it in front of Simon, saying, "Don't be shy now, take as much as you want. Growing boys need to eat. Always have, always will."

"Thanks, Mrs. Morley. It looks so good."

When dinner was done, Marion slid the small box across the table to Simon, leaning back in her chair with a grin. "Have at it, kiddo. Another Edmund Wilder mystery package from the great beyond."

Simon picked up the box, turning it slowly, studying it. The handwriting on the brown wrapping paper was shaky, as if written with a trembling hand.

*To Simon, with best regards, Edmund Wilder*

Kate said, "Open it, don't keep us guessing."

"Fine." Simon was trying to figure out what was in the box. He knew there were six Sacred Rings of Persephone: the Shadow Ring, which he had, and the Illusion Ring, worn by Harrington, the ring allowing him to project his image as an old gardener. Was it possible Edmund had acquired a third sacred ring? It seemed unlikely, since the box was over six inches long, and a ring would only take up–

"Simon?"

"Right, sorry." He pulled on the coarse twine, untying it, then tore off the brown paper, revealing a purple felt-covered rectangular box with a small gold latch.

Kate said, "It looks like a jewelry box. Maybe it's a watch."

Simon unhooked the latch, raising the lid. "It's a brass key and a handwritten note. The key looks really old."

He read the note, then held it up for everyone to see.

WE ARE THE LOST

*In one drop of water are found*

*all the secrets of the oceans.*

Simon set the note down. "What does that mean, and why didn't he say what the key is for?"

Marion said, "Edmund did love his mysteries. I'd love another piece of cake, if you wouldn't mind?"

Harrington cleared his throat. "I believe it is a quote taken from an early twentieth century poet by the name of Kahlil Gibran. He is saying that if you understand the nature of one drop of water, you will understand the nature of all the oceans."

"I get that, but what does it have to do with Wilder House? And who are The Lost? That sounds a little creepy."

Marion shrugged. "Poets, am I right? Those guys always have a few cards missing from the deck. Even more than lawyers." She gave a loud laugh, slapping the table top.

Simon attempted a laugh, reading the note again. Edmund Wilder had purposefully left him another cryptic note and a mysterious brass key. He needed to find out why.

Harrington tilted his head slightly, his eyes on Simon.

# Chapter 4

Simon was relaxing in a pale green wicker chair on the wide covered porch that wrapped around three sides of Wilder House, enjoying the warmth of the early morning summer sun. He stood up when he heard a vehicle coming up the gravel drive, waving when he spotted the familiar blue car with the dented left front fender. It was Clara.

She came to a stop in the circular parking area next to the stone fountain, with its exquisitely carved statue of the Greek goddess Persephone, water flowing from the flask she held in her arms.

Simon ran down the steps to greet her. "Are you ready for some super fun happy skeleton hunting?"

"Let's do it. You have everything we need?"

"It's all down in the storage area."

Five minutes later the two friends were making their way down the back stairs, Simon clicking on the overhead light bulb. "We need to put more lights down here."

"Don't do it, it would ruin the basement's spooky ambiance."

Simon gave her a sideways glance. "Really?"

"Did you bring the ring?"

"It's in my pocket. I don't want to wear it just yet, I want to see the skeleton first. You never did say why we need the metal detector and a shovel."

"To find all the bodies and dig them up."

"What? What bodies?"

Clara laughed. "To look for clues. Who knows what we'll find."

"You can have half of any treasure we find, but any skeletons we find are all yours. That's just the kind of generous guy I am."

Simon eyed the row of closet doors and the piles of furniture sitting in front of them. "I guess we should start with the first door. We'll have to move all this stuff out of the way."

It took almost half an hour to clear away the furniture, Simon stopping to look at an antique desk. "This is kind of a cool old desk."

Clara nodded absently, stepping over to the first closet door. She brushed away a thick layer of dust from the door casing, revealing a brass plate engraved with the number one.

"Edmund numbered the doors."

"Who does that? You have your flashlight?"

Clara clicked her light on.

Simon grabbed the brass door handle, the hinges squealing as he pulled it open, Clara shining her light into the closet.

"Seriously? It's packed with more furniture?"

"If we push those trunks to one side we can get to the back."

Simon sneezed. "This dust is brutal. I should have worn a mask."

When the six trunks had been moved, they stepped to the back of the closet, rapping on walls, looking for hidden switches or levers.

"Nothing here, no secret door, no secret tunnel."

"Let's move on to door number two."

"We can move all the furniture from door two over to door one."

"That works."

They opened the second door, Simon shining his light into the closet. "Seriously? Why did they buy all this furniture? What were they thinking?"

"No idea. We have to move those tables and boxes out of the way."

Simon grabbed one of the wooden crates, almost dropping it when he sneezed again. "This dust is going to kill me. I'll probably sneeze to death."

"I don't think that's a thing."

"It's going to be a thing."

41

Clara squeezed through the remaining furniture to the back of the closet, shining her light on the wall. She rapped on the old wood paneling, stopping when the sound abruptly changed.

Simon grinned. "That has to be it. It sounds hollow."

Clara moved her light across the closet walls and ceiling. "There's a rope hanging down in that corner with a wooden handle on the end. Try pulling on it, see what happens."

Simon pushed his way through to the corner of the closet, climbing over two steamer trunks, then stopped. "We have to be careful, it could be a booby trap, shoots out poison darts like in the movies."

"Pull the rope."

Simon tugged on the rope, the wooden wall panel sliding upward.

"That's it, keep pulling it."

Simon pulled on the rope until it stopped. "How's that?"

"That does it."

"There's a metal ring on the wall, I'll tie the rope to it."

When the door was secured, Clara aimed her light into the darkness. "It's a tunnel. Bingo, Marion was right."

"I'll get the metal detector and the shovel. What do we need the rope for?"

"In case we have to climb down into a cave."

"Just for the record, I'm not climbing down into a cave."

Clara laughed. "I knew you'd say that. So predictable."

The two friends headed into the tunnel, their flashlights illuminating the rocky walls and floor.

"Those support beams are seriously heavy."

"Someone spent a lot of time and money building this."

"The tunnel curves to the right."

"And it's sloping down."

Simon stopped when they rounded the curve, Simon's light revealing a heavy steel door with multiple rows of rivets running across it. "It's just like the door to Edmund's vault room."

They approached the massive steel door, Clara examining it. "I don't see any obvious way to open it."

"What's that X-shaped hole?"

"It could be a keyhole. It's an odd shape for a key though."

"So now we have to find a weird key?"

"What about the key Marion gave you?"

"It's an ordinary brass key, not X-shaped."

"I guess we go back and hunt for a key."

"I'll ask Harrington if he knows anything about the

steel door. Edmund told Marion about the tunnel, so he must have had the key that unlocks the steel door. Maybe he said something to Harrington about it, told him where he kept it."

"It's worth a try. Let's go search his studio. It could be in a desk drawer or something."

"There was a box of old keys in his writing desk, next to my bedroom. Let's check that out, it's where I found the key to the pump house."

"Let's do it."

Simon was turning to leave when he felt the eerie chill roll through him.

Clara stopped short. "Do you feel that? The chill?"

"I do, and it's not the first time. I felt it in my bedroom the other day, and again when I was walking up the hill from the carriage house. It's kind of creepy."

"The chill is following you?"

Simon frowned. He didn't like the idea of being followed by a ghost. "Maybe it's three different ghosts. Why would a ghost be following me? I don't think they do that. Do they? Do ghosts follow people?"

Clara burst out laughing. "You should see your face."

"It's my *holy-crap-a-ghost-is-following-me* face."

Clara snorted. "Put the ghost ring on. Mystery solved. Bada bing."

"I tried that already. Watch this." Simon slipped the

ring on, the chill vanishing.

"I'd say the ghost doesn't want you to see him."

"Or her."

Clara raised one eyebrow. "Or it."

"If you're trying to scare me, it's not working."

"It kind of looks like it is working. Let's go check the writing desk."

They made their way through the basement, heading up the marble stairs to the foyer, then up the grand stairway to the second floor. They methodically searched Edmund's writing desk, then his sitting room and dressing room, but the X-shaped key remained elusive.

"I was sure it would be in that box of keys, or a secret compartment in the desk."

Clara pulled out her phone when she heard it buzz, tapping the screen. "I have to work this afternoon. Someone called in sick."

"I could tell Mr. Fernald you're lost in a secret tunnel under Wilder House."

"I wish. I should go."

"Okay, I'll keep looking for the key. I'll try Edmund's studio."

"Let's go to the movies tonight. There's a new one I want to see called *Forgotten Memories*. It looks really good."

Simon looked notably dubious. "What's it about?"

45

"It's about a woman who has a bad car accident and gets amnesia, then moves back to her hometown. It's gotten great reviews, you'll like it."

"What time?"

"Pick me up at seven. My mom needs her car tonight."

They headed down the grand staircase, Simon walking Clara to her car. "I'll text you if I find anything."

"Text me even if you don't." She put her arms around Simon, giving him a kiss.

"What was that for?"

"For going to a movie with me about a woman who gets in a car accident, gets amnesia, and moves back to her hometown."

"I like being with you, it doesn't matter what we're doing."

"Me too, times infinity."

"I'll walk you to your car."

Simon watched Clara drive off, then headed back down to the basement, continuing the search for the mysterious X-shaped key in Edmund's art studio.

The sun was low in the sky when he finally gave up the search. "There is absolutely nowhere I haven't looked in the studio. The key is not here, it's not in Edmund's writing desk, his sitting room, or the dressing room."

As always, Mrs. Morley served dinner promptly at six o'clock, Simon arriving early, taking a seat at the dining table. He didn't want to be late picking up Clara for the movie.

As they were eating, Kate was looking at him curiously. "You keep looking at your watch."

"I have to pick Clara up at seven. We're going to the movies. I don't want to be late."

Kate smiled. "You can go, I'll tell Mrs. Morley you had a date with Clara. She won't mind, she likes Clara."

"And she wouldn't want me to be late for something." Simon grinned.

"Go."

Simon grabbed his keys and headed down to the carriage house, pulling open the door and hopping into the old truck.

He sped down the gravel driveway, his tires spitting up stones, then turned left onto the highway, one eye on the speedometer. He pressed his foot down, the old engine roaring, the truck vibrating as he raced down the narrow road. He grinned. "Not a cop in sight."

He slowed down as he approached the four-way stop, glancing at the big granite boulder where Jeremiah Davis had met his tragic end. He was wearing the ghost ring, but he drove on through.

"Sorry, Jeremiah, gotta go pick up Clara." He

accelerated, the engine roaring. "I should probably slow down, I'm going way too fast. I don't want to hit a moose like Jeremiah did." He glanced at his watch. It was 6:51. If he hurried they could still make the movie.

He looked in the rear view mirror, his heart almost stopping when he saw the flashing red light in the distance.

"Oh, no! It's a cop, I'm dead, Mom will kill me. And I'm going to be late for the movie. Crap. I can't believe it, I'm going to get a speeding ticket."

He put on his blinker, slowing down, moving over as far as he could onto the narrow shoulder, the pickup coming to a halt. He shut off the engine, reaching for his wallet. He had his driver's license and registration with him, so that was good, but his license was from New York. That would not help matters at all in a town like Caligo Falls. He turned around, his eyes on the bright headlights of the rapidly approaching police car. "He's not slowing down. Wait, maybe he's not after me, maybe I won't get a ticket. He must be after someone else. Sweet."

A chill shot through Simon when he realized the police car was not turning to avoid him. "He's coming right at me!" Simon panicked, giving a screech, trying to slide over into the passenger seat, grabbing at the door. "Stupid seatbelt!" He fumbled at it wildly, trying to unbuckle it, glancing behind him. He screamed when he saw the headlights twenty feet away, almost blinded by the glaring beams. Time seemed to slow to a crawl. He wrapped his arms around himself, hunching down, closing his eyes, bracing for what he knew would come next.

What came next was a dreadful, empty, echoing silence.

Five seconds passed, Simon gingerly opening his eyes. Was he dead? Was this what it felt like to be a ghost? Maybe he hadn't felt the crash that killed him. Could that happen? He looked up, spotting the police car rounding a curve down the road, its red light flashing, watching as it disappeared around the turn.

The good news was, his heart was pounding like a bass drum. Clearly he wasn't dead. But why not? What had happened? Had the police car swerved out of the way at the last second? He would have heard squealing tires, a blaring horn. When he thought about it, he realized he hadn't heard anything. No siren, no racing engine, no screeching brakes, nothing.

It suddenly registered that he'd seen the police car's dark silhouette as it rounded the curve in the road, and there was something odd about it. The car was old, really old, like something in an old gangster movie, like one of the old antique cars in the carriage house.

He absently looked at his hand, gazing at the ghost ring on his finger, a sudden realization occurring. "Holy

49

crap, I think I just saw a ghost car! Is that even a thing?"
He thought about it for a moment. It made sense, he
could see Jeremiah's ghost bicycle, so why not see a
ghost car?

He started the truck, then grabbed his phone, texting
Clara.

*I'm running a little late. I almost got hit by a ghost
car!!*

*What?*

*A ghost police car drove right through my car. It was
terrifying.*

*You're okay? Where are you?*

*I'll be there in ten minutes. I'm fine.*

Clara was waiting on the front porch when Simon
pulled into the driveway. She ran to the truck, hopping
into the passenger seat.

"Tell me exactly what happened, don't leave anything
out."

Simon told her everything, except for the part where
he screamed.

"Do you remember what time it was?"

"It was 6:51. I looked at my watch because I was

50

late."

"You've never seen the car before?"

"Never."

"I don't think it was an accident that you saw the police car. The question is, where was it going, and why was it going there?"

A grin crept across Simon's face. "There's only one way to find out. And for the record, I've always wanted to chase a police car."

# Chapter 5

Simon and Clara were seated in the dining room, Simon drumming his fingers on the polished tabletop. "Okay, where would someone hide an X-shaped key?"

"The most obvious place would be in a desk drawer, or a secret compartment in a desk, but we've search all the desks in the house and found nothing. We found that one secret compartment, but all it had in it was an old checkbook and a pair of glasses."

Simon stopped drumming his fingers. "What about the desks we haven't searched?"

"What do you mean?"

"The key belonged to Cornelius, since he was the one who built the tunnel and the steel door. It didn't belong to Edmund, so maybe we should be looking for a desk that belonged to Cornelius."

Clara looked dubious. "That's all true, but Edmund knew about the secret tunnel and he knew about the skeleton, so he must have had access to the key."

"Maybe Cornelius told Edmund about the skeleton, but Edmund never actually went into the tunnel."

"That doesn't seem like something you'd share with your grandson."

Simon did his best impression of Cornelius Wilder. "Oh, Edmund, if you go into the secret tunnel, just ignore the old skeleton, it's just some guy I murdered."

Clara started to laugh, then grabbed Simon's arm. "It was right in front of us, we already saw it! In the basement, those old desks we had to move to get into the closets."

"Genius! Let's go check them out."

An hour later Simon sank down onto a dusty steamer trunk. "Nothing. Two desks and nothing in them. Zero. Zip. Nada."

"Cheer up, we have five closets left. The desk could be in one of them."

The two friends moved stacks of furniture, travel trunks, lamps and boxes away from door number three. Simon eyed a set of antique golf clubs, brushing the dust off them. "I should take these upstairs. I always thought I'd be pretty good at golf. It sounds kind of fun, walking around on a sunny day, hitting a little white ball across a green–"

"Stay focused, we need to find that key."

Simon pulled on the door to the third closet, the hinges creaking as he pulled it open. He clicked on his flashlight, shining it around the room. "There's a desk in the back, behind those chairs."

They pushed the furniture aside, squeezing their way through to the desk, Clara flicking on her flashlight.

Simon pulled open a drawer. "Empty."

"This one is empty too. Someone cleaned it out."

"Maybe a secret compartment?"

Twenty minutes later Clara shrugged, saying, "No secret compartments. Time to move on to door number four."

When the furniture had been cleared away from the fourth closet, Simon approached the door, pointing to a heavy brass padlock.

"This door is heavier than the others, and it's locked. No way am I searching for a key to unlock a door so I can search for another key to unlock another door. It sounds like a bad video game."

"Fine, let's try door five."

When the fifth door finally creaked open, Simon used his flashlight to illuminate the interior of the closet.

"Bingo. Hello, antique desk."

They searched the desk drawers thoroughly, finding nothing.

"Time for a secret compartment check."

It was Clara who found it when she pulled out a drawer and reached into the empty compartment, feeling around. "There's a little lever in here, I can feel it."

"Pull it."

There was a click, Simon giving a yelp when a wooden panel sprang open. He shined his light into the small rectangular cubby hole. "No key, but there's a little leather notebook. It could be something, maybe a clue."

Clara grabbed the notebook and opened it, Simon shining his light on the faded blue writing. She flipped through the first few pages. "There are lots of numbers with letters next to them. I don't know what it means though."

"Let's take it upstairs and look through it. This dust is clogging my nose up. Does it smell like there's a dead mouse in here?"

"I smelled that too. When's the last time you took a shower?"

"Hilarious, truly hilarious. Let's go."

The headed up to the first floor sitting room, Simon taking a seat on a velvet couch, Clara sitting next to him.

"Okay, the first five pages are numbers with letters next to them, but we don't what the letters mean. Or the numbers."

"Right there, it says *Bay Ridge Savings*."

"Bank accounts! It's a list of account numbers and the name or the initials of the bank next to it."

Clara turned the pages, spotting a list of names with notations jotted down next to them.

Simon pointed to one of the names. "This guy was a senator."

"Here's two congressmen."

"And a judge. And another judge."

"And a senator. What do the notations mean?"

"This one says *800 shares*."

"*1200 shares M&S*."

"Railroad shares! The newspaper article about Tobias Granger said that Cornelius was the owner of the Midland & Southern Railways, M&S."

"I can't believe you remembered that."

"I remember everything, Simon Moody. Everything."

"You're scaring me."

Clara laughed. "Okay, we know Cornelius was giving railroad shares to congressmen, senators, and judges. What does that sound like to you?"

"It sounds like a good reason to hide the notebook in a secret compartment so no one would find out what he was up to."

"He was bribing a lot of important people."

"Exactly. This one says *2000 shares, Chicago route, oil contract*."

"There was a lot of corruption back in the days of the railroad tycoons."

"Some things never change."

"Sad but true. All this is interesting, but it doesn't help

us find the X-shaped key, it only tells us what we already knew, that Cornelius was an unscrupulous railroad tycoon who bribed powerful people to get what he wanted."

Clara flipped slowly through the rest of the notebook, stopping when she reached the inside back cover. "What's that?"

Simon eyed the curious notation. It was written in black ink and circled twice with a red pencil.

*L 32 R 69-3 L 12-3 R*

Clara snapped her fingers. "It's a safe combination! Turn left, right, left, right."

"Did you just snap your fingers?"

"I did. It's what you do when you figure out the answer to a problem, you snap your fingers."

"Like when you shout out '*Eureka*'. Did you know that's what Archimedes said when he stepped into the bathtub and noticed the water level of the tub rose up? He realized he had discovered a way to measure the volume of an irregularly shaped object."

Clara stared at him silently for a moment, blinked once, then said, "Maybe the X-shaped key is in the safe."

"Except I haven't seen a safe in the house. There could be one hidden somewhere though. But where?"

"Well, clearly Cornelius would have hidden it in a very *safe* place."

Simon turned slowly, his eyes on Clara. "A *safe* place?"

Clara gave him a sweet smile.

"You win, best homonym of the day award goes to Clara Barley."

"Thanks. Now we just need to find this mysterious hidden safe."

Simon slumped back against the couch. "This is starting to feel like some crazy never-ending scavenger hunt. Maybe Edmund set this whole thing up to make us go crazy. Or maybe Cornelius did."

"Let's take a break, go do something else."

"Let's try playing golf with those old clubs. It will be fun."

"I was thinking about something a little more exciting, like chasing a ghost police car."

"On second thought, I can play golf tomorrow. How about you stay for dinner and I'll tell my mom we missed the movie last night so we're going tonight, but we have to leave at 6:30. We can have dinner early so we'll have enough time to get to the crossroads and wait for the police car."

"Maybe we should drive farther down the highway and wait for him there."

"Except we don't know how far he went after I saw him. He could have turned after a half mile, or he could have gone fifty miles."

"He had his flashing red light on, so it had to be an emergency. He wouldn't be driving like that for fifty miles."

"He was probably going to the town center."

"How about we drive halfway to town and wait for him there?"

"That works."

At exactly 6:49 that evening, Simon pulled the truck over onto the shoulder of a long straight section of the highway. "We'll be able to spot him from here."

Clara looked back down the highway, watching for the flashing red light. "I have an idea, start driving as soon as you see the flashing red light."

"Why?"

"If we're driving just slightly slower than he is, what happens when he passes through us?"

"We'll have time to see who's in the police car. He'll be sitting right next to us. Brilliant."

"Bingo. You drive, I'll watch."

Simon slipped the ghost ring on, Clara putting her hand on his shoulder.

Simon's hands were on the wheel. "I wonder who's driving the police car? It must be a cop, unless someone stole his patrol car. Maybe there was a bank robbery, and the robber–"

"Simon! I see him! Drive!"

The engine roared, the old truck leaping forward, pushing Simon back against the seat.

"Slow down just a little, let him catch up to us."

Simon glanced in the rear view mirror, the ghost car now fifty feet behind them, its red light flashing.

"Try to match his speed when he's passing through us!"

"Okay." Simon sped up slightly, the police car now only ten feet behind them.

"He's almost here! I'll look, you focus on the driving, try to match his speed for as long as you can."

Simon checked the rear view mirror, the ghost car now only a few feet behind them. "Here he is!"

Clara hollered out, "I can see the driver! It's a policeman!"

Seconds later the ghost car slowly passed through the pickup truck, Clara letting out a scream, trying to jump out of the way.

Simon turned toward her, the truck swerving wildly, the front right wheel hitting the soft shoulder of the highway, spewing up a cloud of dust.

"Follow them!"

Simon yanked at the wheel, getting the truck back on

the road, the police car now fifty feet in front of them. He sped up, jamming the truck into fourth gear, flicking on his headlights, matching the pace of the ghost car.

"Why did you scream? What did you see?"

"It was awful, I think there was a dead guy in the car. There was blood all over the seat and he was slumped over. I couldn't see his face, but he wasn't moving at all. The driver was wearing an old fashioned police uniform, but I was too busy looking at the dead guy to see his face."

Simon's eyes were locked on the speeding ghost car. "We just passed Pine Street, he's going past the town center."

They raced after the police car until it slowed down, making a sharp right turn. Simon followed him, the truck bouncing and shaking as it rolled over chunks of broken concrete.

"Slow down!"

Simon jammed on the brakes, the truck coming to a halt.

They watched as the man in the police uniform leaped out of the patrol car and ran around to the front passenger door, flinging it open. He grabbed the wounded man by the shoulders, dragging him out, then turned, shouting at someone who wasn't there. Ten seconds later the ghost car and its two occupants faded to nothingness.

Simon's heart was still pounding from the rush of adrenaline. "Did you see that? Those bloodstains on the guy's shirt?"

Clara held up one hand. "Shhh!" She grabbed her phone, tapping on the screen, then gave Simon a smug grin.

"What are you doing, why are you grinning like that?"

"No reason, just grinning. I like to grin. It's fun."

"You did something on your phone. What did you do?"

She held up her phone, Simon studying a series of numbers and letters.

*NH 1653 1918*

"What is that?"

"Oh nothing, just the license plate number of the ghost car, a 1918 New Hampshire plate, number 1653."

"No way! You're brilliant! I never even thought about that."

"Thanks. Maybe we can use it to find out who was driving the car. The police must have records of all their old vehicles, hopefully going back to 1918."

"You saw those big bloodstains on the guys shirt?"

"I saw them."

"He totally looked dead when the policeman pulled

62

him out of the car."

Clara's expression was grim. "I know."

"Let's look around, see what this is. I'll leave the headlights on."

Clara climbed out of the truck, scanning the area. "I've driven past here a million times, but I never paid much attention to it. It's a big vacant lot, and it's been here forever, since I was a kid. Do you see any ghosts?"

"No ghosts. That looks like part of an old foundation, and those rusty iron pipes look like plumbing, old water pipes maybe. There was a building here, a big one."

"We need to find out what it was, and why the ghost car stopped here, what he was doing. We can ask around, find someone who remembers what used to be here."

"I'll drop you off at your house. I'll ask Mrs. Morley and Harrington about this place, see if they know what it was."

"I'll ask my mom."

"Oh, don't forget to ask your mom if she knows where the mysterious safe is hidden, and if the X-shaped key is inside it."

"Funny, but kind of obtuse."

# Chapter 6

Simon headed home, parking his truck in the carriage house. He swung the heavy door closed, latching it, then headed up the hill, his thoughts on the dead man Clara had seen in the police car.

The chill hit him as he approached the servants' entrance to Wilder House. He looked around to make sure no one was listening, then said, "Listen, whoever you are, you don't need to hide. You don't need to be afraid of me."

The chill vanished.

"That's a first, a ghost who's afraid of people."

He entered the house, stepping into the kitchen, spotting Mrs. Morley pouring coffee into three porcelain cups on a silver tray. "Hi, Mrs. Morley. Who's the coffee for? Do we have visitors?"

"Marion Jaggers stopped by to see Kate, something about real estate. She wanted Harrington to be there also. She didn't bother calling first, just showed up out of the blue." Mrs. Morley gave a loud sniff.

"I can take the coffee in if you want."

"Good heavens, no, what a thought, Simon Moody serving coffee? Go take a seat at the table, I'll be right in."

Simon walked down the narrow hallway, emerging into the dining room. Kate, Marion, and Harrington were seated at the long table.

Kate looked up when she heard the door open. "Is the movie over already?"

"We never made it. Clara had to do something with her mom, help with something."

"Have a seat, Marion has something to tell us."

"What is it?" Simon pulled out a chair, sitting next to his mom.

Marion pulled an envelope from her coat pocket, setting it on the table. "It's about the land Edmund's great grandfather bought back in 1859."

Kate gave a puzzled look. "What land?"

"Edmund's great grandfather purchased land in 1859 to build a supremely extravagant mansion, flaunting his immense wealth. It was huge, the best of the best, no expense spared, made Wilder House look like a shack. They tore it down in 1931, but the Wilder estate retained ownership of the land, two adjoining city blocks in Manhattan. The land was eventually passed down to Edmund, who leased it out to a number of different corporations over the years. Six months ago we had a generous offer from a buyer who wishes to purchase the land."

Simon's eyes widened. "Two city blocks in Manhattan? How much is that worth?"

Marion reached into her purse, pulling out an Oreo cookie, popping it into her mouth. "So good."

Simon's eyes narrowed.

When she had finished the cookie, Marion grinned, sliding the small white envelope across the table to Kate. "This is their cash offer."

Kate glanced at Simon, then opened the envelope, pulling out a scrap of folded paper. She unfolded it, her jaw dropping. "That's not possible. It can't be."

"Oh, it's definitely possible, and they have the money, it's a verified cash offer. You don't get that every day. I need your approval to sell the land, and I think it's time. The money can be invested in other, more lucrative ventures, if that's what you want."

Kate slid the paper over to Simon. "This should cover your tuition."

Simon gaped at the number. "Nine hundred and fifty-nine million dollars?"

Marion shrugged. "You can get a new pickup truck."

"That's crazy, nobody needs that much money."

Kate said, "I approve the sale, but Simon is right, nobody needs that much money. We'll do something good with it, create a charitable foundation, a trust. I'm not sure what it will be, but we'll do something good with the money."

Marion nodded. "I was hoping you would say that, and I couldn't agree with you more. Edmund would be proud of you and Simon, I know he would."

Harrington nodded his approval.

Marion rose up from her chair, "Gotta go, kids."

Simon said, "Wait, I have a question for you and Harrington. Clara and I drove past an old vacant lot today, about a mile south of the town center. It looks like there used to be a building on it, a big one. Do you know what it was?"

Marion tilted her head, studying Simon. "That's an odd question. Did you want to buy the lot, build a cozy little cottage for you and Clara?"

Simon's face turned a remarkable shade of red. "What? No, that's not it at all, I just wanted to know what the building used to be. Um, I was just kind of curious about the history of Caligo Falls."

"Right, curious about the history of Caligo Falls." Marion looked at Kate, raising her eyebrows.

Kate grinned.

Harrington said, "I am quite familiar with the lot in question, but it was before my time, I assure you. Perhaps you should speak with the county clerk. They would more than likely have a record on file of the property deed for the lot."

Marion pulled another Oreo cookie from her purse. "Good idea, but even better, go ask Bobby at the general store. His family has been here for five generations. He'd know for sure, and no shuffling through paperwork in a dusty old office."

Harrington nodded. "A simple, and yet most efficacious solution."

Marion studied Harrington curiously. "You know a lot of big words for a simple country gardener."

Harrington gave his signature enigmatic smile. "Thank you, madam."

Marion turned to leave, then said, "Come by the store tomorrow, Bobby will be there, he's there almost every day."

Simon rose early the next morning, throwing on his clothes and heading down to the kitchen for breakfast. He pulled out his phone, sending a text to Clara.

*Marion said Bobby will know about the old lot. Can you get off work?*

*Can't do it, busy.*

*Okay, I'm heading over there now to talk to him.*

*Let me know what he says.*

*I will.*

Simon slipped on the ghost ring as he walked down the hill to the carriage house, hoping the mysterious, but shy ghost would finally make an appearance. He backed the truck out, sitting for a moment, the engine idling. "Okay, ghost, be that way. You don't need to be scared of me though, I like ghosts, I have lots of ghost friends."

Twenty minutes later he was pulling into the general store parking lot. He spotted Bobby unlocking the front door.

Bobby stepped over to the truck. "You're here early. Marion called, said you'd be stopping by sometime today. She said you wanted to know about the old empty lot down the road?"

"What did it used to be? There's still part of a foundation there."

"That's where the old hospital was."

"There used to be a hospital there?"

"The first hospital in Caligo Falls. They tore it down in the late 1930s and built a new one, the one we have now."

"Interesting. We were just curious about what used to be there."

"It's just an old vacant lot now."

"I know. I'm kind of interested in the history of Caligo

Falls."

Bobby said, "Lots of history around here. My family's been here for five generations. I take my metal detector around and search for old artifacts, donate them to Mrs. Beasley's museum."

"There's a museum in Caligo Falls?"

"Sort of, it's in Mrs. Beasley's garage."

"Nice. Speaking of metal detectors, would it be okay if we kept yours just a little longer? We haven't had time to use it yet, we had to move around a bunch of stuff in the basement, and we're trying to find a key to open one of the doors there."

"Not a problem. I decided it was time to get a new one. That one is pretty old, and the new models are amazing. It's yours if you want it."

"I'll pay you for it."

"No need, just keep shopping here and eventually I'll get all your money." He laughed.

"Thanks so much. You said your family has been here for five generations? Have you heard any other stories about Cornelius Wilder? I've been trying to find out more about him. I know he wasn't a very nice person, and he was involved in some pretty shady business deals."

"Did Clara tell you anything about my grandfather?"

"Um, she just said your grandfather didn't have a

happy life."

"She's right about that. He was an alcoholic, the local town drunk. He had a lot of demons, but he never talked about them, kept it all to himself. They said he got drunk one night and shot someone, then went home and took his own life."

Simon gulped, no idea what he should say. "Oh, I'm sorry, I didn't mean to bring all that up. I was just curious about Cornelius. Sorry."

"I only mentioned it because the man they said he shot was a friend of Cornelius Wilder."

"Who was he?"

"Not sure, but he must have been a rich guy. Days gone by, best left forgotten."

Simon nodded. "Thanks for the metal detector."

"No problem. Are you getting used to Caligo Falls? It's a big change from New York City."

"I am getting used to it, and I really like it here. It grows on you. I don't miss the city."

"It's a good place to live, good place to raise kids."

Simon nodded. "It is. I should get going. Thanks again for everything."

Simon climbed back into his truck, pulling out his phone to text Clara.

*Bobby said there used to be a hospital on the vacant*

*lot. They tore it down in the 1930s.*

*The cop was taking that guy to the hospital.*

*That has to be it. Bobby told me his grandfather shot and killed a friend of Cornelius Wilder, and then took his own life.*

*No way. Do you think the person he shot was the passenger in the police car?*

*I don't know, maybe. Another piece of the puzzle.*

*We need to find that safe.*

*I'll keep looking for it. Did you ask your mom where it is?*

*Ha ha. The more times you say it, the funnier it gets.*

Simon drove back home, pulling into the carriage house. He climbed out of the truck, his gaze stopping on the wooden stairs that led up to the second floor. "I've never been up there. That looks like a good place to hide a safe. You never know."

He walked up the stairs, eyeing a spider web. "Spiders, so creepy. Someone needs to clean this place, get rid of all the dust and dirt and spider webs."

The second floor was filled with old wooden carriage

72

wheels, harnesses, tires, boxes of car parts, two engines, old car batteries, a pile of old fenders, and half a dozen antique car seats.

"This place is crazy, it's worse than the storage area in the basement."

He pried the lid off a wooden crate, revealing a large pair of old fashioned car headlights. "Whoa, those are crazy old but they've never even been used. Some collector would pay a zillion dollars for those."

Simon studied the dimly lit room, light filtering in through six dusty old four-pane windows, an acrid musty smell permeating the air.

"So much old stuff here. This must be where they kept the spare parts for their cars and the old horse drawn carriages. This all belongs in a museum."

Simon strolled around the room, tapping on the walls, looking for a hidden safe. "Nothing, no safe here."

He idly brushed a thick layer of dust off one of the grimy windows, peering outside at the spruce trees below, eyeing a narrow dirt road running down the hill.

"I never noticed that old road. I wonder where it goes? I should check it out."

He spent a half hour poking through old car parts, then headed back outside, squinting in the bright sunlight.

He strolled around to the back of the carriage house, heading down the narrow dirt road. He was rounding a turn when he spotted the long low shed, its roof covered with a layer of moss.

"Whoa, that's not too creepy looking. Probably fifty ghosts in there with big ghost knives." He felt for the ghost ring in his pocket, deciding not to wear it until he'd inspected the shed, until he knew what was in there.

He approached the old building, studying it. "It's bigger than I thought, and it has the same kind of doors as the carriage house, so it must have been built around the same time. Maybe this was the first carriage house, and then they built a bigger one. Or maybe they kept the horses here."

He raised the heavy iron latch, pulling the door open, the hinges squealing, something scurrying across the floor, Simon jumping back. "That looked a lot like a raccoon. Great, I'll probably get eaten by raccoons and no one will ever know what happened to me."

The floor of the shed was lined with straw, but the elephant in the room was a very large object covered in a crusty old stained canvas tarpaulin. "That looks like a car, a big one."

He reached for the corner of the tarp, then stopped. Suppose the car was filled with raccoons, a whole family of them. That would not be good. Taking a deep breath he grabbed the tarp, wiggling it, waiting for a dozen angry raccoons to leap out. They didn't, so he pulled the tarp off, stopping when he saw the old car.

"It's the car from the photograph! The one with Cornelius and his chauffeur, Tobias Granger."

He walked around the vehicle, examining it. It was incredible, there was some dust and dirt, a bit of rust, but all in all it was in amazing shape. He opened one of the doors, looking inside, expecting to see mice living in it. "No mice, no raccoons." He picked up a pale blue card sitting on the front seat, recognizing Edmund's handwriting.

*1917 Rolls Royce Silver Ghost, four speed transmission, 7.4 liter, six cylinder. Purchased new by Cornelius Wilder in 1917*

"I can't believe it's the same car. This is so cool." He stepped on the running board, climbing up into the driver's seat, putting his hands on the large wooden steering wheel. "No power steering back then, you had to be strong to drive a car like this."

He realized he was sitting exactly where Tobias Granger used to sit, his hands on the polished wooden steering wheel. He turned, looking back at the dusty leather seats. That's where Cornelius Wilder used to sit. How amazing was this? He frowned when the eerie chill rolled through him. Seconds later it was gone.

"That was weird. And not in a good way. Maybe the friendly ghost is stalking me."

He hopped out, pulling out his phone and taking a picture of the Rolls Royce, sending it to Clara.

*Like my new car?*

*What is that??*

*It's the car Cornelius Wilder bought in 1917, the one in the old newspaper photo. I found it in an old shed about a quarter mile down from the carriage house, covered with a tarp. It's in great shape for being that old.*

*That's incredible! I can't wait to see it!*

*No safe yet. I looked up in the second floor of the carriage house. Zip. Nothing there except for a zillion dollars worth of old antique car parts.*

*Keep looking. I'll come by after work.*

*See you then. Miss you.*

*Miss you too. Don't open the safe if you find it. I want to be there.*

*Okay.*

*I mean it. Do not open it.*

*Fine, I won't, I promise.*

# Chapter 7

Simon walked slowly up the hill to the house, hoping he'd feel a chill, hoping the timid ghost would reveal itself. He took a stroll around the outside of Wilder House, the ghost remaining elusive. He glanced up at the widow's watch on the peak of the roof. That was where he'd first seen Darlene Morley's ghost, spotting her floating above the lake. The locals called it Ghost Lake, and Marion said she'd seen a ghost there, a blue translucent form.

Simon and Clara had never told anyone about the conversations they had with Darlene after Robert Sawyer had helped her to wake up, the two friends learning the truth about how she had tragically drowned.

He rounded the house, stepping into the gardens, the grounds meticulously cultivated by Harrington over the years, many of the flowers and trees brought back from other countries by Edmund Wilder. Simon spotted Harrington clipping dead blossoms off a cluster of bright yellow flowers.

Harrington turned, greeting Simon. "A lovely day for

a stroll."

"It is. I was just down at the old shed on the dirt lane past the carriage house."

"Ah. I assume you saw the old Silver Ghost? It belonged to Cornelius Wilder. Edmund was quite fond of that old car."

"I saw it. It's amazing, it must be worth a billion dollars."

"Quite a tidy sum for a pile of rusted metal, glass and old leather."

Simon was silent for a moment, then said, "You're saying it's just stuff, it has no intrinsic value?"

"Quite so, it is a physical object residing in an illusory world, and to complicate matters even more, it is composed of nothing more than compressed energy, a concept which effectively renders all physical matter objectively non-existent."

"An illusory world?"

"Reality is fluid, ever changing, impossible to grasp. I think you already know this."

"That's all true, but it's still a really cool car."

Harrington smiled. "Excellent. One must play in the dream, that is why we are here."

"Right, play in the dream. So, I never know if I should I call you Claudius or Harrington."

"It would be best to always call me Harrington, we

wouldn't want to confuse anyone who happened to over-hear our conversation."

"Good point. I was wondering, did Edmund ever say much about Cornelius Wilder?"

"He spoke of him from time to time, but there was no fondness to be found in his memories. At an early age his grandfather mandated that he be sent off to a notoriously strict boarding school, Cornelius perceiving Edmund to be too gentle, too kind. To survive in this world he believed one needed to be hard, tough, merciless. Cornelius said the school would turn Edmund into a man."

"That's awful. He must have had a really unhappy childhood."

"Quite so. Whether or not his parents disagreed with Cornelius I do not know, but they were nonetheless forced to submit to his demands. He was very persuasive, as you might well imagine."

"What was the school like?"

"He seldom mentioned it, but he did say once that the students were severely beaten for the slightest infraction of the rules, and they were instructed to report the infractions of other students or they themselves would be equally punished."

"They spied on each other?"

"As you can well imagine, it was a most unpleasant environment for Edmund. It says a great deal about him that out of such a harrowing childhood he emerged as a kind and empathetic man."

"I wish I could have known him."

"You have much in common with him. You would have been good friends had you known each other."

"Did he like being rich?"

"He deemed it to be a heavy burden, a responsibility, a weighty anchor that tied him to this world, but also one which allowed him time to do the things he loved."

"Like painting?"

"Precisely. He was happiest when he was standing in front of an easel."

"Or talking to the ghost of Emma."

"Perhaps that most of all. She was the love of his life. It is curious that you should be such a good friend to Clara, Emma's granddaughter, almost as if history is repeating itself."

"I know, we've talked about that. Don't tell anyone, but Clara says she doesn't want to make the same mistake Emma made, leaving Edmund behind when she went off to New York to start her own real estate business."

"Perhaps it was not a mistake at all, perhaps it was simply a necessary lesson to be learned by Emma. I foresee a marvelous life together for you and Clara."

"I like her a lot."

"I can see that you do, your face changes when you talk about her."

"Oh, I had a question. We found a little notebook in a desk down in the basement. On the back page someone had written the combination to a safe. Do you know anything about a safe in the house? It didn't say where it was or what was in it, just the combination."

Harrington tapped his lips, thinking. "Edmund never mentioned a safe, and I have never seen one. That being said, there could be one hidden somewhere in Wilder House, perhaps put there by Cornelius or Edmund's father."

Simon's phone beeped. It was a text from Clara.

*Did you find the safe yet?*

*No, I didn't find it. I haven't started looking in the house yet.*

*Did you find the safe yet?*

*Yes, very funny. Ha ha.*

*Yes, you found it?*

*NO NO NO I did NOT find it.*

*Ha ha ha. I get off early today, I'm coming by to help you look for it.*

*Help me look for what?*

*Did you find the safe yet?*

Simon burst out laughing. Clara was hilarious. He glanced at Harrington. "Um, just a funny text from Clara."

Harrington smiled. "All is right with the world."

Simon headed back into the house, searching through Edmund's studio again, looking in all the closets, behind the racks of paintings, anywhere a safe might be hidden. He finally gave up, returning to the front porch, waiting for Clara to arrive.

He stood up when he heard her car coming up the driveway, waving to her. She pulled into the parking area, jamming on the brakes and jumping out of the car, hollering, "I know where the safe is! I know where it is!"

Simon ran down the steps. "What? How did you find it?"

"Well, I don't know exactly where it is, but I know where it is."

"That makes no sense."

"Imagine you're watching a movie about a super rich guy living in a giant mansion, and he just wrote a new will that he's going to hide in the safe because he's disinheriting his lazy slacker son but he doesn't want him to know about it yet."

"Have you been drinking?"

"Do it, just imagine it."

Simon closed his eyes. "Fine, I'm a super rich guy living in a giant mansion and I have a new will that I'm going to hide in the safe so my slacker son won't–" He stopped short, a light blinking on in his head. "It's behind a painting! Why didn't I think of that? It's always behind a painting in the movies. They swing the painting open, and boom, there's the safe."

Clara laughed, grabbing his hand. "Let's go check those paintings."

The two friends stepped into the magnificent foyer of Wilder House, Simon immediately eyeing the large austere portraits hanging on the wall next to the grand staircase.

"It's probably not hidden behind one of those big paintings, too hard to get to. You'd need a step ladder."

"It also wouldn't be behind any of Edmund's paintings, since he painted them long after Cornelius or his father installed the safe."

"True. So we're looking for an easily accessible, average sized painting, most likely one commissioned by Cornelius or his father."

"Let's start in the basement and work our way up to the third floor."

They found one old painting of Cornelius' mother on the wall of the art studio, but there was no safe behind it. "Let's check the other rooms down here: the study, music room, and the exercise room."

A quick stroll through the rooms revealed no paintings with a connection to Cornelius.

"I'm starting to think Edmund wasn't very fond of Cornelius."

Simon nodded. "You got that right. You should hear what Harrington told me about Edmund's childhood. Not a fun time, they sent him off to some crazy strict boarding school where they beat you if you broke the rules."

"That's awful."

"I know. Let's try the first floor."

They headed up the marble stairway to the atrium, spending almost an hour going through all the rooms: the billiard room, smoking room, dining room, sitting room, a drawing room, library, parlor, and two studies.

Clara said, "Who cleans all these rooms?"

"We hardly ever use them, mostly just the dining room and the sitting room. And the bedrooms. We take turns vacuuming every few weeks, do some dusting."

"Sounds like a lot of work."

"They used to have as many as two dozen servants living here, keeping everything clean, polishing the silver, doing all the laundry, cooking, stuff like that."

"Must have been nice."

"Not for the servants. You can imagine how Cornelius must have treated them."

"Good point. Let's go upstairs."

They walked up the grand staircase to the second floor sitting area, Clara eyeing the velvet window seat. "It was so amazing that I got to talk to Emma when she was still here."

"I'm glad she and Edmund are together, wherever they are."

Clara took his hand. "I'm glad we're together, wherever we are."

"Floating around infinite space on a giant ball of rock?"

"So romantic."

Simon was about to reply when he spotted a painting nestled between two tall bookshelves. "There, that has to be it! It's Edmund's grandmother, it's the right size, and it's easily accessible."

Clara darted over to the painting. "Can I do it?"

"Go for it."

Clara grabbed the right side of the painting, glancing at Simon. "Ready?"

"Yes, I'm ready, just do it."

"Are you absolutely certain you're ready? You're not just pretending to be ready?"

"Do it!"

Clara pulled on the painting, giving a yelp when it swung open, revealing an old iron safe behind it. "We found it."

"How cool is that?"

"What's the combination?"

Simon pulled the small leather notebook from his pocket, flipping to the back cover, reading the combination to Clara. In less than a minute there was a soft click. Clara pulled the handle down, swinging the heavy safe door open.

She took a step back. "Is that…"

"It's a gun, an old revolver. We shouldn't touch it, fingerprints." Simon shined his flashlight on the weapon, studying the writing stamped into the side of the gun. "It's a Colt Model 1917, .45 caliber."

"It's the right time period, it must have belonged to Cornelius."

Clara pointed to an old box of bullets. "The bullets are the same caliber as the pistol."

Simon carefully reached into the safe, feeling around, giving a triumphant yelp when he reached behind a heavily lithographed tin box. "No way!"

He pulled out a black iron key, holding it up for Clara to see.

"The X-shaped key! You found it!"

"I don't believe it, we actually found the key. This is incredible."

"What's in the tin box? It looks fancy, all those floral designs printed on it."

"Maybe it's an old chocolate box. They used to be really fancy." Simon took it out of the safe, gently removing the lid. "Old photographs, really old ones, lots of them."

"Let's look through them, maybe we'll find something."

"Maybe we'll find a photograph of Cornelius murdering someone in the secret tunnel."

Clara gave him a sideways glance, picking up the box, carrying it over to the window seat, Simon sitting down next to her.

Simon picked up the first photo, studying it. "Whoa, I think that's Woodrow Wilson. He wore those weird glasses."

"How do you know that?"

"History class?"

"Cornelius Wilder knew Woodrow Wilson. That's crazy."

They sifted through several dozen more photos, none of the faces looking familiar, but they did recognize some of the names written on the backs of photos: Rockefeller, Vanderbilt, Carnegie, and numerous senators and congressmen.

"They all look rich. Look at that mansion, and that car. It looks kind of like the Rolls Royce Silver Ghost."

"We should search the car in the shed for clues. Were you wearing the ghost ring when you found it?"

"No."

"Why not?"

"It was already creepy enough with the big raccoon. I didn't want to risk it, maybe get brutally murdered by a family of ghost raccoons."

"You are amazing in so many ways."

Simon grabbed the next photo. "Here's one of Cornelius standing next to a guy with a fancy suit and a big mustache. It doesn't look like that guy ever missed a meal." He turned the photo over, reading the handwritten notation on the back.

*Partner, F. Thornton, NYC July 1910*

"That's interesting, it's Cornelius and his partner in 1910. We should research it, find out more about him."

Simon was studying the photo of Cornelius and his partner, his brow furrowed. "His partner looks familiar. I feel like I've seen him before, that big mustache, but I don't know where. I'll go through Edmund's newspaper articles again, see if I can find him. Kind of a cool mustache. Maybe I should grow a big mustache."

"It's funny you should mention that, because I just read an interesting article saying girls never kiss guys with big mustaches."

"And, checkmate."

# Chapter 8

The next afternoon found Simon behind the wheel of his truck, driving down the narrow highway toward the town center, the bright summer sun streaming into the truck's cab, the ghost ring's green gem sparkling in the sunlight. He had decided to wear the ring when they investigated the tunnel, especially since Marion told him the tunnel was haunted, possibly by the ghost of whoever had been murdered.

He rolled to a stop at the crossroads, spotting Jeremiah Davis riding his antique high-wheeled bicycle, the Penny Farthing. He drove on with a quick wave to Jeremiah, in a hurry to meet Clara. As he was approaching the town center, however, something caught his eye, something that made him stop.

"No. Way. I don't believe it."

Simon pulled over to the side of the road, his eyes on the ghostly figure standing in front of a freshly painted pale yellow house.

A split second later the ghost was sitting in the truck next to Simon.

"Hey, cowboy. How's tricks?"

It was Robert Sawyer, the doctor who had been murdered by his wife Bertha.

Simon said, "What are you doing here? I thought you
went to Paris to see the Eiffel Tower?"

"Been there, done that. Traveled all over Europe.
Rode my bike."

"Ghosts can ride bikes?"

"Remind me again, what's that thing Jeremiah Davis
is riding?"

"Right. Wouldn't it be easier just to fly around like
ghosts are supposed to do?"

"Not the same, bucko. Best way to see Paris is riding
a bike, suck up all that delightful French ambiance."

"I guess. Where else did you go?"

"South of France, Spain, Italy. Hit all the big land-
marks. The Colosseum in Rome was fun, talk about
haunted, so many angry ghosts with swords sticking out
of them. Hilarious, half of them didn't know they were
dead, still trying to fight each other."

"That doesn't sound hilarious, it sounds more like the
worst nightmare you could ever have. You did all that in
two weeks?"

"Hey, are you still friends with that little cutie pa-
tootie?"

"You mean Clara?"

"That's the one. She break your heart yet? Crush your dreams into a pile of dust?"

"No, she's kind of my girlfriend now."

"Kind of?"

"She is my girlfriend. We're both going to college in Boston this fall. Different schools, but they're close to each other so we can see each other."

"Word of advice, if you get married, make sure she doesn't murder you. It can happen, they do that. Murder you for your money. Like Bertha did."

"I know that, I know she did. Don't forget, she's in prison now, paying for what she did to you."

"Oh, I haven't forgotten, trust me on that. I go laugh in her face every few days. She can't see me, but my therapist says it could help me with my deep-seated intimacy issues."

Simon blinked. "You have a therapist?"

"Why wouldn't I?"

"A ghost therapist?"

"Of course she's a ghost. I met her in Paris at a little cafe. You can't walk ten feet in that town without bumping into a bunch of jabbering ghost tourists."

"Is that like a ghost who's a tourist?"

"It's not *like* that, it *is* that. It's not all just creepy dead guys haunting old amusement parks and scaring teenagers, there are plenty of regular folks who led busy lives, never got the chance to see Paris. Like me, for instance, thanks to Bertha. Speaking of that crazy bitch, a new family moved into my house, painted the place. Looks nice, doesn't it? I like them, it's nice to hear kids laughing, playing, the parents not screaming at each other, threatening to call the police, smashing dishes, trying to poison each other. I always wanted kids, but Bertha always wanted money."

A wave of sadness rolled through Simon. He wasn't sure what to say, so he changed the subject, trying to lighten the mood. "You must have met some interesting people in Paris."

"You got that right. I met a guy who flew to the moon, said it was interesting, but not a lot to do there. Duh. Sounds boring to me, sitting on the moon watching all the morons on Earth stomping around spewing out insipid comments and murdering each other."

Simon raised his eyebrows. "You might want to consider spending a little more time with that therapist."

"Hey, you should be a therapist, so perceptive, spotting my unresolved anger issues like that. Just FYI, my therapist says I'm doing great. She met Carl Jung in 1934, so you know she's good. She wasn't a big fan of Freud though, said he was a weirdo. She's also hotter than a flaming tamale in hell. That's a win-win in my book."

"I don't think you're supposed to say things like that about your therapist."

"You haven't seen her, cowboy. Yowza."

"On a completely different topic, can I ask you something?"

"Knock yourself out. It's about girls, right?"

"No, not about girls. I saw a ghost police car driving down the highway toward Caligo Falls. A cop was driving and maybe there was a dead guy in the passenger seat."

"Old news, seen it a hundred times, cruises past here every evening."

"It drives past your house?"

"Every evening, like clockwork. Some rich guy in a fancy thousand dollar suit got himself shot in a police car, three bullet holes through the windshield. Poor sap, a lot of good all his money did. What a moron."

Simon turned at the sound of a screen door squealing open, two children dashing out of the house. They were laughing, one of them holding a colorful beach ball, tossing it into the air.

Robert's expression changed, his face softening. "I wish I was like that, could laugh and play. The world changes you, rips away your innocence, bashes you in the head with a big club."

"It doesn't have to."

"You sound like Dorothy. She keeps telling me bad things are good things in disguise, you learn from them, evolve. Maybe it's true, I learned a lot from being murdered by Bertha the Bitch."

"Who's Dorothy?"

"My super hot therapist. Speaking of which, I gotta go meet her. We're having lunch at a little cafe on the Rue de Champs-Élysées."

"Sounds romantic."

Robert grinned and winked at him. "You got that right. See you around, cowboy. Don't get murdered." He vanished in a blink of light.

Simon sat silently after Robert was gone. He didn't want the world to change him, he didn't want to be angry like Robert. Dorothy was right, bad things were usually good things in disguise. When his mom told him they were moving to Caligo Falls, he thought it was the worst thing that had ever happened to him, but then he met Clara.

Simon thought about it, realizing that moving here hadn't been the worst thing that had ever happened to him. The worst thing was when his dad ran off with his secretary, leaving Simon and his mom to fend for themselves.

Meeting Clara had changed everything, transforming the move to Caligo Falls into the best thing that had ever happened to him. He was surprised by how much Clara's friendship was helping him to cope with his dad leaving. Her parents had gotten divorced when she was in the seventh grade, a devastating event in her life. They talked about it a lot, how it had changed their lives, the sadness and the anger. She said it was good to talk about things like that, not just keep those painful feelings bottled up inside you.

He put the truck in gear, heading down the road toward Pine Street. He couldn't wait to tell Clara about Robert, that he had a therapist, a ghost therapist. How crazy was that? The world was getting stranger every day.

Clara was waiting for him outside the grocery store. She hopped into the truck, leaning over and giving him a hug. "Where were you?"

"I stopped to talk to an old friend."

"Old friend? Who?"

"Robert Sawyer."

"He's back from Paris?"

"He is. And he has a therapist who's hotter than a flaming tamale in hell."

Clara laughed. "I think you'd better tell me the rest of that story."

Simon laughed.

An hour later the two friends were walking down the

back stairs of Wilder House on their way to the basement. Simon jumped when he saw something dart across the room. "What was that?"

"What? What did you see?"

"I don't know, I saw something though. It wasn't very big, but it moved fast."

"Like a mouse? Are you wearing the ghost ring?"

"I am wearing it, and it was definitely not a mouse." He handed Clara one of the flashlights, stooping down to pick up the metal detector and the shovel, approaching the second closet door, trying his best not to imagine what a hundred-year-old skeleton would look like, big vacant eye sockets and grinning yellow teeth. "This is going to be scary."

"Not for a brave paranormal investigator like you."

"Oh, right, I forgot how brave I was."

They stepped into the closet, Simon pulling on the rope in the corner of the room, the door sliding upward.

Clara clicked on her flashlight and the pair entered the darkened tunnel, finding their way to the mysterious riveted steel door.

Simon took out the black X-shaped key. "Are you ready for this?"

"Do it."

"Are you absolutely certain you're ready? You're not just pretending to be ready?"

"Are you hijacking my joke?"

Simon inserted the key, twisting it, hearing the familiar whine of an electric motor, the heavy steel door sliding open.

"That was easy." Simon shined his flashlight into the tunnel, studying the massive wooden support beams. "I wish I knew what he did here. It took some pretty serious engineering to build this."

"I'm not sure I want to know what he did in here."

"Good point. It slopes downward, kind of steep, then turns to the right."

They rounded the curve in the tunnel, Clara being the first one into the secret room. "Twelve-foot ceilings at least, this is big."

"I don't see a skeleton." Simon was studying a jumble of empty wooden crates lying on the right side of the room. The opposite wall was lined with heavy iron shelving, currently empty.

"Whatever he kept on those shelves is long gone." He approached the pile of wooden crates, examining one of them. "They're old whiskey crates, there must be twenty of them at least. Maybe Cornelius was a bootlegger during prohibition."

"Or he just liked whiskey." Clara moved her light across the back of the room. "Skeleton! Over there, near the wall."

Simon saw the bones, stepping slowly toward them, his anxiety rising. "His clothes are decayed, almost gone, but not his boots. You could dust them off and they'd look almost new."

"He's lying on his stomach."

"Pretty sure he doesn't have one of those anymore."

The skeleton's arms and legs were at odd angles, the bones separated, the muscle and cartilage that once held them together long gone. The skull was face down in the dirt, Simon glad he didn't have to look at the gaping eye sockets.

Clara said, "You should see the look on your face."

"I guarantee it's better than the look on the skeleton's face. It's creeping me out, it used to be someone, they used to be alive, walking around doing stuff, now he's just a big pile of creepy bones."

Clara nodded, kneeling down next to the skeleton, studying the bones. "All true, but only part of his story. Look how the ribs are shattered here and here. He was probably shot. Maybe with the gun we found in the safe."

She stood up, reaching for the metal detector.

"What are you trying to find?"

"I don't know yet." She clicked it on, moving the detector slowly across the dirt floor, listening to the barely audible humming noise. She stopped moving it when it made a loud squeal.

"Dig there. Carefully."

Simon used the shovel, gingerly digging into the earth, rewarded by the sight of a heavy lead bullet. "Got it. You were right, he was shot."

Clara carefully wrapped the bullet in a tissue without touching it, putting it in her pocket. They found a second bullet a few minutes later, next to the wall. "This one must have gone right through him and hit the wall."

"Good to know, right through him. Should we do anything? With the skeleton?"

"We shouldn't move anything, it's a crime scene. We'll need to contact the police. They can tell us if the gun in the safe is the one used to kill him."

"I don't want to call them just yet, I want to find out more about what happened here. Do you notice anything unusual about the skeleton?"

"He's huge?"

"So was Cornelius' chauffeur. He was big, six-foot-five at least, maybe taller, and in the photograph he was wearing tall leather boots like these ones, part of his chauffeur's uniform."

"You're saying you think Cornelius killed his chauffeur?"

"Kind of looks like it. His name was Tobias Granger."

"Any ghosts here?"

Simon shook his head. "None. Maybe Tobias moved

on."

Clara looked doubtful. "Maybe, but it seems strange that he's not here, not haunting the place where he was murdered."

They walked slowly around the room, searching for more clues. "I wonder why Cornelius didn't bury the body? He just left it here."

"It's the perfect hiding place, probably no one knew about the tunnel, and he kept the only key to the steel door locked in the safe."

"Is that a door?" Simon stepped over to the far wall, pulling on a small brass handle, a narrow wood panel creaking open. "More tunnel, it slopes down, it's steep."

"Let's see where it goes."

"Should we get the rope?"

"We'll be fine."

"Said the captain of the Titanic."

Clara snorted.

They made their way down the silent murky tunnel, stopping when they reached a rusty iron ladder leading up to a wooden trapdoor.

Clara turned to Simon. "Any ghosts yet?"

"No."

Clara climbed up the ladder, raising the trapdoor, light flooding into the tunnel.

"Where are we?"

"In the boathouse, down by the lake."

"That's crazy, there's a secret tunnel from the house down to the lake."

"Perfect for smugglers or bootleggers. Bring the whiskey across the lake in a boat, then take it up to the house through the tunnel. Who knows what else they were up to; they could have been smuggling anything."

"Maybe Cornelius caught Tobias stealing his whiskey, and that's why he killed him."

"That's not much of a reason to murder someone."

"True, he would have just fired him."

"It must have been something really serious to make Cornelius murder him."

"Maybe he knew too much. In the movies, people who know too much always get murdered."

"In this case, you might be right. Maybe Tobias found out something really bad about Cornelius; maybe he was blackmailing him."

# Chapter 9

It was the middle of the night, the ghostly chill worse than it had ever been. Simon shivered, pulling the blankets tightly around him, but it didn't help, if anything, the chill was getting worse, his teeth chattering. His room was an empty black void, the very definition of darkness, Simon filled with an overwhelming sense of dread.

There was something in the room, he could sense its presence, something he didn't want to see. He gingerly reached over to the bedside table, feeling for his phone, terrified that something horrible, something with claws, was going to grab his hand. He pulled the phone back to his bed, tapping on the flashlight, moving the beam around the room. There was nothing, only the eerie shifting shadows from his light.

The ghost ring was sitting on the bedside table next to his lamp. If he put the ring on and turned on the light, he would see what was in the room. Or, maybe the chill would vanish when he put the ring on. He could almost hear Clara's voice, "Just do it, Simon. See what it is."

He gave a silent groan, shutting off the phone's flashlight, reaching for the ghost ring, slipping it onto his finger. The chill was still there, it hadn't vanished. Whatever was causing it was here, waiting for him. He took a deep breath, letting it out slowly, trying to calm himself. He was being silly, letting his crazy imagination run wild. If he turned on the light, what was the worst thing that could possibly happen? Wrong question, he didn't want to know what the worst thing was. He had to stop thinking, he was making himself crazy, he had to just do this, get it over with, rip off the band-aid.

In a single fluid motion he reached over and flicked on the bedside table light, letting out a piercing shriek when he saw it, slamming backwards against the headboard, banging his head.

There was a boy sitting on the end of his bed.

Time came to a screeching halt, Simon's eyes locked onto the translucent boy. He was holding a toy wooden horse, playing with it, making it jump back and forth. It was like that scary movie, the one with the ghostly twin girls in the hallway. *Come and play with us. Come and play with us.* He was feeling lightheaded, ready to take the ring off.

And then he recognized the ghost.

"It's that kid from the photograph in the servants' quarters, down in the basement. He had a wooden horse

105

just like that one."

The boy seemed blissfully unaware of Simon's presence, his focus directed on the toy horse as he made it hop around. Simon's fear was diminishing rapidly, now that he had identified the ghost as a known quantity. It was a child, and to be truthful, his presence was now more sad than scary, a small boy all alone in a huge old rambling house, playing with a small carved wooden toy horse.

Simon attempted a friendly, casual tone. "Hello, there, I like your toy horse. It's really nice."

There was no response from the boy.

"Did someone give you the horse? Maybe for your birthday?"

The boy, the horse, and the chill abruptly vanished, Simon staring at the empty space where they had been. This was an unexpected turn of events, a child haunting Wilder House. What had happened to him? Why was he still here? Where were his parents? They should have come back for him, helped him move on.

He lay back down, closing his eyes, sleep eluding him for almost an hour, the boy's ghostly image burned into his memory.

He awoke the next morning, sunlight pouring into his room, the chill gone. He grabbed his phone, texting Clara.

*I saw the ghost last night, the one who was following me. It's the little boy from the old photograph in the servant's room in the basement. He was sitting on the end of my bed, playing with his toy wooden horse.*

*That makes me want to cry. Did you talk to him?*

*I tried to, but he vanished. I don't know if he could hear me.*

*He used to vanish when you put the ring on, but he didn't vanish this time. Maybe he's not as scared of you now, that's why he's showing himself. He's probably still afraid to talk to you, still checking you out. When you feel the chill, talk to him, but be gentle, say nice things so you don't scare him.*

*I tried that, but he vanished. I wish we knew more about him. Like what happened to him, where his parents are.*

*I feel so bad for him, he must be so lonely. He's been there for over a hundred years.*

*I know. I hardly slept last night. I'll try talking to him, see what happens. Maybe he can tell us his name.*

Simon got out of bed, pulling on his clothes, stepping over to the window. He gazed out across the estate, his thoughts still on the ghost boy. Had he died in the house? How? Maybe he didn't want to know how. Maybe it was something horrible.

"I need to take my mind off this, think about something else." He glanced around his room, spotting the velvet jewelry box that Marion Jaggers had given him.

"I still don't know what that old brass key is for, or why Edmund gave me the quote about the drop of water and the ocean."

He opened the box, staring at the antique brass key, studying it. That was the moment the light of recognition blinked on, Simon remembering the padlock on the closet door in the basement, the fourth door, the one they had passed over because it was locked. Maybe this was the key to the brass padlock.

He sent a quick text to Clara.

*The brass key Marion gave me might be for the padlock on the fourth closet door in the basement.*

*Try it, but don't look inside yet, wait for me. I'll come by after work. Don't open it. Do NOT open it.*

*Okay, I won't open it. You don't need to say it again.*

*I'm not saying it, but I'm thinking it. Now I'm thinking it again.*

Simon burst out laughing. Clara was so funny. He grabbed his flashlight and ran down the grand staircase to the foyer, stopping when he saw Harrington step through the front door carrying a blue cut glass vase filled with colorful flowers.

"A fine good morning to you, Simon."

"Morning. What are the flowers for?"

"For the upstairs sitting room. Edmund liked to have fresh cut flowers there, he said they brightened up the room, though I suspect they were for the benefit of his beloved Emma. I thought it might be a nice gesture, it's been a long time since I put flowers there."

"That does sounds like something Edmund would do. Oh, I think I might know why Edmund left me that brass key. I'm going to go check on it now."

"Ah."

Harrington's monosyllabic reply struck Simon as both curious and telling. Why hadn't Harrington asked him what the key was for? That's the first question most people would have asked. Did he already know what it was for?

Simon said, "I think it's for the fourth closet door in the basement. That's the only door that was padlocked."

Harrington nodded, his expression unchanged. "Remind me again what the note said?"

Simon knew Harrington had not forgotten what the note said, but he took it out anyway, reading it, *"We are the Lost. In one drop of water are found all the secrets of the oceans."*

"Most puzzling indeed."

Simon had a feeling that Harrington did not think it was puzzling at all.

"I'll let you know what I find out."

"Excellent."

Simon ran down the marble stairway two steps at a time to the basement, making his way to the back hall of the house. He stopped at the room with the framed photograph of the boy, stepping into the shadowy interior, picking up the photo, studying it closely. There was no doubt about it, this was absolutely the boy who was sitting on his bed. He flipped the frame over, looking on the back. Nothing there, but maybe someone wrote something on the photograph, something that would identify the child.

Carefully removing the cardboard backing, Simon slid the old yellowed photo out of the frame, eyeing the barely legible pencil written words.

*Frankie, 1917, Wilder House*

The boy's name was Frankie. This was good, he would use his name the next time he talked to him, treat him like an old friend. He slipped the photograph into his pocket, entering the storage area, flicking on the single overhead bulb.

He turned on his flashlight, winding his way through the piles of furniture and boxes to the fourth closet door. Taking Edmund's brass key from his pocket, he inserted it into the lock, hesitated, then turned it, rewarded by an eminently satisfying click, the lock popping open.

"No way, it worked!" He removed the padlock and grabbed the door handle, stopping when he remembered his promise to Clara, that he would not look in the room until she was with him. He waited for almost a full minute, trying to rationalize his next move.

"I won't go into the room, I'll just take a quick peek, open the door just a crack. I'm not wearing the ghost ring so I won't see any ghosts, if there are any in there. Clara would do the same thing if she were here. Just a quick peek, that's all, nothing more, no matter what I see. Quick peek, close the door. Boom. Done and done."

He pulled the door open another inch, shining his light into the darkness. This closet was far larger than the other ones, extending back at least twenty feet. It was also completely empty. That was unusual, the other closets

111

being packed with old furniture.

"Why would it be empty? Why would Edmund give me the key to an empty room?" He opened the door a little wider, setting one foot in the room. It wasn't as empty as it had first appeared, there was a long wooden rack lining the far left wall, the rack filled with unframed canvases.

Simon gave up any attempt at rationalization, entering the room and stepping over to the rack of unframed paintings. He pulled one of the canvases out, studying it. It was a landscape, clearly done by Edmund, but the colors were odd, and the trees didn't look right. Maybe he was experimenting with a new style of painting, using a different palette, some kind of abstract modern art look.

Nevertheless, the question still remained, why did Edmund leave him the key to this room, and what did 'We are The Lost' mean? The paintings were lost? That made no sense at all. Simon's eyes widened when he reached an inescapable conclusion. There was something in this closet that was only visible when he was wearing the ghost ring. And maybe it was something very bad.

He backed slowly out of the room, closing the door behind him, locking it. He definitely wanted Clara to be with him when he wore the ring in there. He didn't want to see whatever it was by himself, especially something called the Lost.

His phone beeped as he was ascending the marble stairs, a text from Clara.

*You looked in the closet, I know you did.*

*Why would you say that?*

*Because I would have looked. What was in it?*
*Spill it, Simon.*

*Fine, I just took a quick peek. It was empty except for a rack of unframed paintings by Edmund. I don't think he liked them, they were painted in a weird different style, odd colors.*

*Were you wearing the ring?*

*No way, I'm waiting for my paranormal investigative partner. Just in case.*

*Good. I'll stop by tomorrow afternoon. I had a genius idea, BTW. Possibly the best idea in the history of best ideas.*

*What kind of genius idea?*

*We know where the police car went, but where*

*was it coming from?*

*Whoa, that is a genius idea. If we track it back to where it came from, we can find out where the murder took place.*

*Exactly. See you tomorrow!*

Simon frowned, giving some further thought to Clara's plan. If they found out where the murder took place, they might have to witness the murder. That was a not a very appealing scenario.

He decided to find Harrington and ask him about the fourth closet and the rack of paintings. He suspected Harrington wanted him to figure all this out on his own, but it was worth a try.

He was strolling along the wide covered porch when the chill hit him again, worse than ever, like walking through an invisible wall of ice. He stopped, feeling for the ring in his pocket, gripping it tightly. "So cold."

Pulling two wicker chairs together, he took a seat in one of them, leaning back and closing his eyes, shivering. After a minute he slipped the ring on without looking at the other chair, his eyes still closed. The chill had not vanished.

"Frankie? Is that you? It's a lovely day, isn't it? Nice

114

and sunny."

Simon turned slowly, trying not to react when he saw Frankie sitting in the chair next him, holding his toy horse.

Frankie looked up, briefly making eye contact with Simon, then lowered his head again, studying his toy horse.

"It's nice to see you again, Frankie. I get kind of lonely here in this big house. My mom is here, and Harrington and Mrs. Morley are here, but I don't have any friends to play with. My best friend Clara comes over to visit sometimes though. She's really nice, you'd like her a lot. She loves kids."

Frankie's voice was barely a whisper. "Are you my papa?"

Simon blinked. This was unexpected. "No, I'm not your papa, Frankie, I'm just a friend. I was hoping maybe we could play together sometime."

Frankie vanished.

Simon slumped back in his chair. Not all that he had hoped for, but it was definitely a breakthrough. Frankie had talked to him. Now he had to find out why Frankie was in Wilder House a hundred years after he had died, and why he thought Simon might be his papa.

# Chapter 10

Clara brushed her hair back with one hand as they drove down the narrow highway. "Robert said the police car passes by his house every evening?"

"Like clockwork."

"How are we going to track it back to where it came from?"

"We keep going farther and farther down the road each night until we spot it. It probably came out of a driveway, maybe a side road. It can't be that far."

"Let's find a long straight section of road so we have a good view. You're wearing the ring?"

"I am. How about there, the road up ahead is straight for a least a half mile."

"Perfect."

Simon pulled the truck over, shutting off the engine and the headlights.

"It's getting dark, the sun's going down."

Simon glanced over at Clara, grinning. "It is kind of dark and scary here, I might need a hug."

Clara laughed, sliding over next to him, taking his hand so she could see the ghost car, leaning her head against his shoulder. "Eyes on the road, we don't want to miss the car."

Simon checked his watch. "It's 6:34. We know the car passes the crossroads at 6:47, thirteen minutes from now, and the car is traveling about sixty miles an hour, one mile every minute. We're twelve miles from the crossroads, so it should pass here anytime now."

Clara sat up suddenly, pointing down the road. "Simon! There it is! It came out of a side road!"

"Keep your eyes on the spot where it came out."

Simon started the truck, putting it into gear, heading down the highway, taking a quick glance at the ghostly police car as it flashed past them.

"Keep going, it was near that bunch of tall trees on the left."

"Tell me when to stop."

"Here, pull over here."

Simon stopped the truck on the gravel shoulder, eyeing the group of tall trees on the other side of the highway. "Where's the road? I don't see a road."

Clara shook her head. "I don't know, that's where the car came out, I'm sure of it."

"Let's go look."

The two friends climbed out of the truck, clicking on their flashlights, crossing the highway. "I don't see a road, just trees."

"Wait, we're forgetting that the murder happened over a hundred years ago. The trees have all grown up, no more road."

"You're right. And the ghost car can drive through the trees, it doesn't need a road." Simon stepped a few feet into the dense forest, shining his light at the ground. He kneeled down, brushing aside a thick layer of pine needles and leaves, giving a triumphant shout. "Gravel! This used to be a gravel road."

"What now?"

"We mark the location on my phone and come back during the day, see what's down the road."

"Once we find something, we can come back a half hour or so before the police car leaves."

"And witness the murder?"

Clara scrunched up her face. "Maybe you could watch it and tell me what you saw."

"Not a chance, brave paranormal investigator."

Simon drove Clara home, then headed back to Wilder House.

When he stepped into his bedroom, he saw the very last thing he was expecting to see, Frankie sitting on the bed. Simon gave a silent groan. He was exhausted, just wanted to crawl into bed and go to sleep, but that wasn't going to happen.

"Hi, Frankie, it's nice to see you. Thanks for coming

to visit."

Frankie floated down to the floor, looking up at Simon. "Will you wake my mama?"

Simon's insides twisted like a bag of hungry snakes.

"What?"

"I can show you."

Simon had no idea what was happening. "Where is your mama? Do you talk to her?"

Frankie shook his head, looking down at the floor.

"No, sir."

"Is she in the house?"

"In the woods."

A crushing fear rolled through Simon. "She's in the woods?"

"I don't like it there."

"But you want to go there?"

"Mama is sleeping in heaven. The man told me."

"What man?"

"I don't know."

"It's dark out, maybe we should go tomorrow, during the day."

It was the first time Simon had ever seen a ghost cry.

"Mama."

Simon felt awful, this was the saddest thing he'd ever seen. He had to do something, he had to help. "Okay, we can go. I have a flashlight so we can see. Is it far?"

Frankie wiped his eyes. "I don't know."

"You don't know?"

Frankie shook his head.

"Okay, lead the way. I'll follow you." Simon grabbed his flashlight, fairly certain he was making the worst decision of his life, walking into the woods at night with a ghost boy who probably had no idea where he was going, trying to find his mother who had died a hundred years ago.

Fifteen minutes later he was making his way through the dark forest, Frankie a few feet ahead of him.

Simon let out a screech when a large insect flew into his face, flailing wildly at the buzzing creature. "Gahhh! Get away!"

He had to run to catch up to Frankie, pushing through the dense forest, the pine needles jabbing his arm. "Frankie, are we almost there yet? How much farther?"

There was no answer, Simon watching Frankie walk through a huge pine tree, disappearing into the forest.

"Frankie, where are you?" Simon's anxiety spiked. "Frankie? Are you still there?"

"I found Mama."

If Simon could have had one wish, it would be that Clara was standing next to him. Everything was so much scarier when he was alone, but here he was, and he had no choice. He pushed on through the trees, emerging into a clearing, his heart sinking down to the center of the earth when he saw the gravestones. This was great, now he was in a graveyard, in the dark, in a creepy forest, accompanied by a ghost looking for his dead mother. The graveyard was old, really old, moss and lichen covering the crooked gravestones, thick weeds growing up around them, his flashlight sending low eerie shadows across the cemetery.

"Frankie?"

"Mama is sleeping in heaven."

Simon saw Frankie on the far side of the graveyard standing in front of a tombstone. He walked past the graves, noting the dates carved into the simple stone markers. All of the people here had died in 1918. He glanced around, looking for ghosts, seeing none. He kneeled down next to Frankie, shining his flashlight on the gravestone.

*Rose Doyle*
*Loving mother of Frankie Doyle*
*1891 - 1918*

Simon looked at Frankie. "Your mom's name was Rose?"

Frankie pointed to the gravestone. "Mama is sleeping."

"She's in heaven. She would be here with you if she could, but heaven is too far away, she can't come back no matter how much she wants to."

Frankie put his arms around the gravestone. "Can you wake Mama?"

Simon moved his light beam, illuminating the small gravestone next to Rose's. He felt sick when he read it. Really sick.

*Frankie Doyle*
*Beloved son of Rose Doyle*
*1912 - 1918*

Frankie had died when he was six years old, the same year his mother had died. Simon got to his feet, saying, "We should go back to the house now. It's late, we need to go. We can come back here again in the daytime if you want. We could bring some nice flowers for your mom."

"I have to wait for Mama."

Simon shook his head. "I'm so sorry, but she can't come back, Frankie, she's in heaven now. I can't wake her."

Simon instinctively held out his hand for Frankie, forgetting for one brief moment what happened when he touched a ghost. Frankie grabbed Simon's hand.

There was a sudden blink of light and the forest was

gone, the cemetery was gone, replaced by the inside of a swaying carriage holding almost a dozen men, women, and children, a sunlit forest passing by on either side of them. Simon looked down at his legs, he was small, wearing short gray pants and worn brown leather shoes. He was holding his mother's hand, feeling anxious and excited.

The carriage came to a stop a few hundred feet later, a tall man wearing a top hat and a long black jacket with tails approaching the carriage, opening the door.

"Welcome to Wilder House. Collect your belongings and follow me, if you would. You will be shown to your quarters and informed of your duties at Wilder House."

Simon looked up at his mom, his eyes wide. "Is that our house?"

"No, sweet one, this is Wilder House, it belongs to the master of the house, Mr. Cornelius Wilder." She leaned down, whispering, "He's as rich as a king, maybe richer."

Simon stared at the house, his eyes on the gleaming luxury touring car parked next to the stone statue of Persephone. He recognized it instantly as the car he had discovered in the old shed behind the carriage house, the 1917 Rolls Royce Silver Ghost.

This was not the first time Simon had experienced the memories of a ghost, but it was an unnerving sensation to have his own consciousness merged with another. He was simultaneously Simon Moody and Frankie Doyle, seeing Wilder House through the eyes of a child in 1917.

Rose held his hand, helping him climb down from the carriage, Frankie unable to take his eyes off the enormous house with its turrets and widow watch so high above him. He tugged his mom's hand, whispering, "Who is that man?"

"He is one of Mr. Wilder's butlers. He's helping us."

The group of newly hired household help followed the butler around to the back of the house, entering into the back hall, walking down the stairs to their new quarters in the basement, the butler motioning for Rose and Frankie to enter a small room with a cot, wardrobe, and dresser.

"A second bed will be provided for the child. Your quarters shall be kept in a clean and orderly state at all times, according to the rules of the house. Sloppiness will not be tolerated. Any infraction of the house rules will result in a summary dismissal."

He studied a small leather notebook, running his finger down the page. "Ah, here it is, Rose Doyle and one child. Your position is that of chambermaid. You shall be provided room and board, a uniform, and a monthly payment of ten dollars and sixteen cents. You may unpack your belongings now. Mrs. Watson will be by shortly to apprise you of your duties. The child will be attended to on the third floor by the under nurse during your working hours. You will not set foot in the front hall outside of working hours, and you will speak only when spoken to. Is this clear?"

"Yes, sir."

"Very well, you may proceed." The man turned and left, Simon looking up at Rose. "What did the man say?"

"A nice lady will watch you while I clean the rooms. And we get ten dollars every single month. Soon we'll be as rich as Mr. Wilder." She laughed, rubbing Simon's head. "Now, help Mama unpack, we have to hurry, Mrs. Watson will be here shortly."

The room swirled and vanished, Simon feeling a painful tightness in his chest. He was coughing, he couldn't stop, he was so cold, shivering. He was lying on a narrow white cot, his head turned to one side, his eyes on a group of frightening people wearing white coats and masks, walking around the room, stopping at the cots, wiping foreheads with a damp cloth, giving people water. He was scared, he didn't understand what was happening. Several dozen cots were lined up in three rows, the canvas tent filled with the sound of coughing, gagging, people gasping for air. He looked at the cot next to him, his mama looking back at him.

"It will be all right, Frankie. I promise you, we'll get better." Her skin was a frightening shade of blue.

She turned away, coughing violently, her body convulsing.

Frankie had no idea what was happening, but Simon knew. It was 1918, and all the people lying on the cots, many of them that same sickly blue color, were deathly ill. Simon was trying to breathe, his chest tight, his body trembling. He knew that everyone who was buried in the small cemetery had died in 1918, the year of the great pandemic. They had called it the Spanish Flu, but there was nothing Spanish about it, it was a new and deadly strain of the influenza virus, killing millions of people across the world. He'd read about it in history class, never considering how terrifying it must have been for people at the time. He looked over at Rose. She wasn't moving. A nurse was pulling a white sheet over her.

"Mama? Mama?"

A man in a white coat leaned over Simon, resting his hand on his shoulder. "Your Mama is sleeping in heaven, child. I am sorry. She was very ill, but she has found her everlasting peace. You may take heart in that."

Simon was gasping for air, his eyes on the cot next to him, the tent growing darker by the second. "Mama?"

There was a flash of bright light, and the tent was gone, Simon back in the graveyard, Frankie standing next to him.

Frankie and his mom had died in the 1918 pandemic,

and they were both buried here, along with a few dozen other people, household staff from Wilder House.

"Let's go, Frankie. We can come back here again. We'll bring some flowers, maybe trim the grass a bit. You can stay in my room if you want."

"Will you be my papa?"

"Okay, but just for a while."

Simon was eyeing Frankie, noticing that the chill he had always felt in Frankie's presence was gone. He wasn't sure what it meant, but it seemed like a positive development.

An hour later Simon was lying in his bed, sending a text to Clara.

*You're NOT NOT NOT going to believe what happened!*

*Why are you up so late?*

*Why are you up so late?*

*I couldn't sleep, I keep thinking about the murder we might see.*

*I know what happened to Frankie. I know how he and his mom died.*

127

*How do you know?*

*I followed Frankie into the woods because he wanted to show me where his mom is. I was freaking out, so scary. There's an old graveyard about a quarter of a mile back, a bunch of people buried there who died in the 1918 pandemic. His mom's name was Rose Doyle. Her gravestone was next to his. They both died on the same day.*

*You went to a graveyard in the woods in the middle of the night???*

*It was terrifying.*

*You really are a brave paranormal investigator. Did Frankie tell you what happened to them?*

*He grabbed my hand in the graveyard.*

*You relived his memories?*

*It was awful. I didn't think anything could be that sad. He watched his mom die, and then he died. It was so bad.*

*That's awful. Why is he still here?*

*He's waiting for his mom. He thinks she's going to wake up.*

*Oh, no. Can we help him?*

*I don't know, I told him he could stay in my room for a while. He wants me to be his papa. I said okay but just for a little while.*

*You're such a sweetheart.*

*I know you are, but what am I?*

*Remind me again how old you are?*

*Ha ha. Did you find the safe yet?*

# Chapter 11

"I still haven't decided if this ring is a curse or a blessing." Simon glanced over at Clara, his hands gripping the steering wheel.

"Maybe it's both."

"You're right, any great gift is usually a curse and a blessing. Like me being so handsome, for instance, girls always looking at me, asking me out. It's so annoying."

Clara snorted. "You're the one who's a curse and a blessing. But mostly a blessing." She patted his shoulder. "We're almost to the turnoff, I can see the tall trees."

"Park over there and we can hike down the old gravel road, see what we find. You have the ring?"

"I do, but I'm not wearing it. I'm not in the ghost hunting mood right now, not after what happened last night. The cemetery was brutal, the tent with all those sick people in it, and watching Rose die, feeling how scared Frankie was."

"I'm sorry you had to see that."

"I'm sorry Frankie had to see it. It doesn't seem fair, he was just a kid and he had to watch his mom die."

"He probably didn't understand what was happening, he was only six years old."

"I hope you're right." Simon pulled over onto the shoulder, shutting off the engine. The two friends walked across the highway, stepping into the shadowy pine forest.

"You can still see gravel where the road used to be." They walked for almost half a mile, Clara spotting a dilapidated old shack, a section of the roof collapsed.

"The road ends here. This wasn't a road, it was a driveway."

"I wonder who used to live here?"

"Let's check it out, look for clues."

They approached the house, Simon peering in through a cracked dusty window into the shack's murky interior.

"It's old, no electricity and no plumbing."

Clara pointed to a derelict outhouse leaning to one side, the splintered door lying on the ground, partially hidden by tall weeds, insects buzzing around it. "Need to use the bathroom before we go?"

"I'd rather be eaten by weasels, but thanks anyway." Clara laughed.

Simon stepped up to the front door, twisting the knob, pushing it, jumping back when the door toppled over into the house, sending up a cloud of dust and debris.

"Definitely a fixer upper. What do you think, should

we make an offer?"

"It is tempting, but I'm going to have to go with an all caps NO."

Simon entered the shack, scanning the interior. "Lovely, a classic nineteenth century one-room dilapidated shack, fully furnished with a broken bed, smashed lantern, rusted wood stove, doorless antique ice box, a three-legged kitchen table, and a dresser with one drawer missing. Plus an added bonus, a badly stained throw rug that has seen better days. I'm thinking mice, lots and lots of mice."

"Look around, see if you can find any papers that will identify the owner."

"Check out all the beer cans. I'm guessing a lot of teenagers used to party here."

Clara was rummaging around in a dresser drawer. "Found something!" She held up an old torn envelope.

"Is that a letter?"

"Just an envelope, but it's addressed to someone named Josiah Finch."

"Finch? Why does that sound familiar?"

"Bobby's last name is Finch. It could be a relative."

"Maybe it's his grandfather. This place looks old enough for it to be. Whoa, I wonder if this is where he took his own life? That's seriously creepy, but it kind of makes sense, another piece of the puzzle."

"You could put your ring on and find out for sure why we're here."

"No thanks. Not happening. Not after last night."

Clara put her arm around him. "I know you're worried about Frankie, but I'm sure we can help him find his mom. We can do it. Don't let it upset you."

"I couldn't do this alone, you know. It was awful without you at the cemetery, but I'm glad you didn't have to see everything."

"I couldn't do this without you either. It's hard to see some of the things that happened in the past, the things that turned people into ghosts."

Simon nodded. "We're a good team, Moody and Barley Paranormal Investigations. Moody and Barley."

"I'm going to ignore that for now, but let's come back here around 5:30. We can use the ring and find out what happened."

Simon looked around the interior of the shack. "It doesn't make sense."

"What doesn't?"

"Robert Sawyer said the man who was shot in the car was wearing a fancy thousand dollar suit. Why would a crazy rich guy be visiting an old destitute alcoholic living in a one room shack?"

"That is a good question. Maybe we'll find out tonight. We don't know for certain that the man in the car was shot here. Let's go to your house, I want to see the cemetery. Frankie can come with us."

"I told him we'd bring his mom some flowers. Harrington will give us some."

Much to Simon's surprise, Harrington had no knowledge of Frankie or the old cemetery, but was happy to give them a lovely bouquet of flowers to put on Rose's grave.

Frankie followed them through the forest, walking next to Clara, looking up at her and smiling.

Simon whispered, "I think he likes you."

They set the flowers on Rose's grave, Clara kneeling down next to Frankie. "Your mom is in heaven, and she can't come back here to be with you, but when you're in heaven you know lots of things. She knows that you brought these pretty flowers for her, and she knows how much you love her. She loves you more than anything in the whole world, and she would come back if she could."

That was the moment Simon decided that Clara was the most amazing person he'd ever met. Ever.

Mrs. Morley fixed them an early dinner, Simon saying they were finally going to the movies. An hour later the truck was parked on the side of the highway, Simon and Clara standing next to the old decrepit shack belonging to Josiah Finch.

Simon glanced at his watch, slipping on the ghost

ring. He reached out and took Clara's hand. "It shouldn't be long now, a few minutes at the most."

They spotted the ghost police car driving toward them through the dense forest, coming to a stop near the old shack. The car door swung open, a police officer climbing out.

Simon whispered, "No flashing red light."

They watched as the uniformed man crept silently to the house, peering inside through a small window, then reached over, gingerly turning the knob and easing the door open a few inches, looking inside.

Simon and Clara stepped over to the window.

"There's a guy lying on the bed. He's sleeping. It must be Josiah Finch."

Clara pointed to two empty whiskey bottles lying on the floor next to the bed. "I don't think he's sleeping, I think he passed out. Bobby said he was an alcoholic."

Simon's eyes widened when he saw the police officer pull a heavy revolver from his coat pocket, the man's cold eyes on Josiah Finch. Before Simon and Clara knew what was happening, he stepped over to the bed and fired a single shot from the revolver, the brilliant flash lighting up the interior of the shack.

Simon let out a screech. "He shot him! He shot Josiah Finch!"

The policeman put the gun in Josiah's lifeless hand,

135

pressing Josiah's fingers against the grips of the gun, then pulled it away, dropping the gun on the bed.

The man scanned the room, picking up a whiskey bottle, setting it on the bed next to Josiah. He looked around for almost a minute, then strode out of the house, closing the door behind him. A minute later he was driving through the trees toward the highway, the police car's red light flashing.

Simon and Clara stood in stunned silence, beyond horrified at what they had just seen.

Simon shook his head in disbelief. "He shot Josiah Finch, he murdered him, a cop did it."

"And he made it look like a suicide. Josiah Finch didn't kill himself."

"Why? Why would a cop do that? Why kill him?"

"I don't know, maybe Josiah knew something, maybe he saw something?"

"We need to find out more about the policeman, who he was, what happened to him."

"And if it wasn't Josiah, then who shot the man in the thousand dollar suit? And where did it happen?"

"All good questions, ones we have to find answers to."

Back in the truck, Clara turned to Simon, saying, "You know what we have to do now, don't you?"

Simon sighed. "I'm guessing it has something to do

with ghosts?"

Clara nodded. "And?"

"And reliving their memories?"

Clara nodded again. "First we have to find the ghosts.

I have a feeling the murder of the chauffeur and the murder of the man in the thousand dollar suit are connected, and more than likely Cornelius Wilder was involved in both murders. We have to figure out how and why those two men were murdered. We need to relive their memories."

"I just had a thought."

"What?"

"Maybe the ghost of the chauffeur is in the fourth closet, the one with the weird paintings. Maybe he was shot there, then dragged into the tunnel."

"I guess that's possible, but why shoot him there, and what about the bullets we found in the secret room?"

"I don't know, it was just a thought."

"I'll come by tomorrow and we can use the ring, find out exactly what or who is in the fourth closet."

"What about the note Edmund left for me? It didn't say anything about a murder, just a quote about a drop of water and the ocean."

Clara shrugged. "Harrington did say Edmund loved his mysteries. I'm sure we'll figure out what he was trying to tell us."

"The license plate!"

"What license plate?"

"The one from the police car. We should go to the police station and see if they have a record of it. I'll make up a story about an antique Caligo Falls police car that I saw in a magazine. I bet we can find out the name of the policeman who was driving it."

"You're right, we have to do that first. If we can get his name we can go to the Caligo Falls Gazette and search for old articles about him, maybe about the shooting, and find out who Josiah Finch was supposed to have murdered."

# Chapter 12

Simon and Clara decided to postpone their visit to the fourth closet while they researched the license plate number of the ghost car, hoping to discover the identity of the police officer who was driving it on the night that Josiah Finch was murdered.

"Okay, here's the plan, we go into the police station, ask them about the old license plate. They probably have wooden racks in the basement filled with hundreds of dusty old file boxes we'll have to sort through."

"That sounds a lot like a scene from an old mystery movie. They have a montage of the detective searching through old files, drinking lots of coffee and yawning, stretching, then giving a shout when he finally finds something."

"Quite true, but personally, I think it would be kind of fun to hunt through old files in the basement. And, as you said, we'd have to drink a lot of coffee."

"Do you drink coffee now?"

"No, but I'd have to drink it while we were searching through the old file boxes. That's how it works."

Clara rolled her eyes, pushing open the door to the police station, stepping inside.

Simon's gaze landed on a lone police officer leaning back in his chair, feet up on his desk, his face hidden behind a magazine. This was definitely not NYPD.

Clara gave a friendly smile, calling out, "Hi there, we were wondering if you could help us?"

The policeman didn't look up. "Did someone get murdered?"

"What?"

"Just kidding. Your cat is stuck in a tree, right?"

"No, we're trying to get information about an old license plate that we think was on a Caligo Falls police car back around 1918."

The officer lowered his magazine, looking at them curiously. "Who are you?"

"I'm Clara Barley and this is Simon Moody, Edmund Wilder's nephew."

"You're related to Edmund Wilder?"

Simon nodded. "My mom inherited Wilder House. We used to live in a tiny apartment in Brooklyn." Simon didn't want the police officer to think he was a spoiled rich kid.

"I always heard Wilder House was haunted. And those stories I heard about Ghost Lake, very spooky. You couldn't pay me to live there. You see any ghosts?"

"No, nothing like that, it's just a big old house."

"They say people liked Edmund, that he was a bit quirky, being an artist and all, but he donated buckets of money to the town. He probably paid for half the equipment in the police department. What's the plate number?"

Clara pulled the scrap of paper from her pocket. "It's NH 1653 1918."

Simon couldn't help himself, blurting out, "I saw it in a magazine about old cars."

The police officer looked up at Simon. "You saw it in a magazine?"

Simon panicked. Suppose the cop asked him what magazine it was? This was not good. He had to change the subject. "So if you have a bunch of old file boxes in the basement or something, we'd be glad to help search through them, trying to find the plate."

"We don't have a basement."

"Right, well, in the back then? They always keep the old boxes of files in the back, at least in the movies. They search for hours, drinking coffee and then–"

Clara kicked Simon's leg.

The officer laughed. "You've been watching too many old movies. All the archives were digitized about five years ago. No dusty old boxes, no searching for hours, no drinking coffee. I'm Sergeant Rogers, by the way." He studied Clara's face. "I think I know your mom. She's Sarah Barley, right? I gave her a speeding ticket about two years ago."

Clara grinned. "My mom got a speeding ticket?"

"I probably shouldn't have said that. Let's see if we can find that plate for you." He tapped on his keyboard, scrolling through pages of data, finally stopping. "You said 1653, a 1918 plate?"

"That's it."

"The car was purchased in 1917 by Police Chief Walter Merrick as his personal patrol car."

"Does it say what happened to the car?"

"It does. It was sold in 1926 to a C.Whitaker and D.River for $950."

"That's amazing. Thanks so much." Clara jotted the names down next to the license plate number on the scrap of paper. "Oh, just to clarify, since it was his personal patrol car, Chief Merrick would be the only person who drove it?"

Sergeant Rogers gave Clara a curious look. "That's an oddly specific question."

"I was just curious, that's all. It would be kind of fun to know who used to drive it."

The sergeant turned to Simon. "I was a homicide detective in Chicago before I decided to move to the sleepy little town of Caligo Falls. I'm going to go way out on a limb and say you didn't see that plate in a magazine. Why are you interested in it? Where did you really see it? Why do you care who was driving it?"

Simon was a deer in the headlights. "Um, it's kind of a long story."

Clara jumped in, rescuing Simon. "You're right, he didn't see it in a magazine. He saw it somewhere else. Do you believe in ghosts?"

Sergeant Rogers blinked, looking over at Simon, then back to Clara. He pointed to the door. "Have a nice day."

Clara grinned, heading for the door.

When they were back in the truck Simon said, "Well played, paranormal investigative partner. Thanks for saving me, I had no idea what to say."

"The odds are that Police Chief Walter Merrick was driving the ghost car, and he was the one who murdered Josiah Finch."

"That's crazy, the Caligo Falls Police Chief may have murdered Josiah. We need to research Chief Merrick, find out more about him. Let's go to the Caligo Falls Gazette and check out their archives."

"You mean hunt through racks of dusty old file boxes in the basement?"

"We could do that, of course, if we wanted to. We could also search the newspapers online archives, probably a lot quicker."

Clara laughed. "You have a laptop, right?"

"Back at Wilder House. Let's go check it out."

As they were driving, Clara searched on her phone for the local paper's website. "Got it, Caligo Falls Gazette."

"Do they have archives of their old papers online?"

"They do, but you have to subscribe to the paper to read them."

"A paywall, that's so annoying. How much is it?"

Clara stared at Simon.

"What? Why are you looking at me like that?"

"How much is it? Said the bazillionaire who lives in a gigantic Victorian mansion filled with gold coins and jewelry."

"I know, it's dumb, but I can't get used to having money. We had to count every penny back in Brooklyn. I still worry about how much things cost."

"It's not dumb at all. I totally get it." Clara tapped her phone. "Boom, we're good to go, you're a subscriber. You can reimburse me; I take cash, credit cards, ancient gold coins, or priceless jewelry."

"Wait, I have to reimburse you for the subscription? That doesn't seem fair, shouldn't we split the cost? When I think about it, it was your idea, so you should pay for all of it."

Clara gave a start, her eyes wide. "Simon, I just had a vision, a scary one. A ghost is going to visit you tonight."

144

"What ghost? Why do you look like you're going to laugh?"

"You will be visited by the Ghost of Christmas Past, Ebenezer Moody."

Simon burst out laughing. "Gold medal for that one." Twenty minutes later they were in the first floor sitting room, Simon tapping on his laptop. "What's the password for the Gazette archives?"

"BAMPI."

"What's BAMPI?"

"It's an acronym."

Simon furrowed his brow. "I give up, an acronym for what?"

"Barley and Moody Paranormal Investigations, it rolls off the tongue. BAMPI. BAMPI. It's fun to say, unlike MABPI."

"I'm going to ignore everything you just said." Simon entered the password. "Okay, we're in. I'll search for Walter Merrick, see what pops up."

Clara leaned over, studying the screen, frowning. "Those are all current references, definitely the wrong Walter Merrick. This Walter Merrick is alive and owns a furniture store."

"I'll try Josiah Finch, 1920s murder, Caligo Falls."

A single article appeared, Clara grabbing Simon's arm. "That's it! We found it!"

*April 12, 1923*

## *HORRIFIC SHOOTING NEAR CALIGO FALLS*

*A most dreadful and lamentable occurrence took place ten miles north of Caligo Falls on the evening of April 11, casting a pall over our tranquil community. Mr. Josiah Finch, in a state of evident intoxication, staggered onto the highway into the path of a police patrol car operated by our esteemed Police Chief, Mr. Walter Merrick, who stopped his vehicle to avoid colliding with Mr. Finch.*

*In a shocking and unprovoked act of violence, Finch, brandishing a revolver, discharged three shots through the windshield of the police vehicle. The bullets found their mark, fatally wounding Mr. Frederick J. Thornton, a distinguished gentleman from New York City, who was accompanying Chief Merrick to the train station. Mr. Thornton, known for his close association with the illustrious railroad magnate Mr. Cornelius Wilder, succumbed to his injuries almost instantly.*

*Chief Merrick, displaying commendable composure under such duress, positively identified Mr. Finch as the assailant. The Police Chief's account of the incident describes Finch as being in a deplorable state,*

146

*unsteady on his feet and clearly under the influence of alcohol. This tragic event was made all the more grievous by the senselessness of the act.*

*Upon receiving word of the shooting, a contingent of officers swiftly surrounded Finch's home, only to discover that Mr. Finch had ended his own life. The revolver, which had also claimed Mr. Thornton's life, lay upon the bed beside an empty bottle of whiskey, a silent testament to the night's grim proceedings.*

*Mr. Thornton, by all accounts a man of substantial repute and connections, will be sorely missed. Mr. Wilder, who had counted Mr. Thornton among his closest confidants, has expressed profound grief at this untimely loss.*

Simon's mouth was hanging open. "That's why the guy in the police car looked familiar! Frederick Thornton was in one of the newspaper clippings, standing in front of the Rolls Royce Silver Ghost, the guy with the big mustache."

Clara said, "Now we know. Josiah Finch was framed by Police Chief Walter Merrick for the murder of Frederick Thornton, Cornelius Wilder's business partner."

"And if it wasn't Josiah Finch who killed Thornton, then who was it?"

"And why did they kill him?"

Simon closed his laptop, rubbing his chin. "I've been thinking about it a lot, and I'm pretty sure I know who did it."

"Who?"

"The butler did it. In the old detective movies it's always the butler, because he's the one you never suspect; he just walks around in the background and no one pays any attention to him."

Clara gasped, clapping her hands together. "Case closed, the butler did it! Let's crack open a bottle of champagne!"

Simon laughed. "But on the off chance that it wasn't the butler, maybe we should talk to a few ghosts, do some more digging."

"My first ghost choice would be Frederick Thornton. He could tell us for certain if Walter Merrick shot him."

"My first ghost choice would be Tobias Granger, Cornelius Wilder's chauffeur and bodyguard. He was murdered here in Wilder House, and he would definitely know who shot him. My guess is Cornelius Wilder, but I don't know why."

"We could tell the police about the skeleton in the tunnel. They could run tests, compare the bullets we found in the secret room to ones fired from the revolver in the safe."

"Still too soon. Even if it is the gun that shot him, it

doesn't tell us who fired it, or why. Maybe it wasn't Cornelius."

"True."

"It's possible that Thornton and Granger's ghosts may have both moved on."

"Or they haven't. They may have stayed behind until their murders are solved, the same way Robert Sawyer wanted you to prove that Bertha poisoned him."

"Where do we start?"

"How about the fourth closet? That could be where Tobias was murdered."

"Let's do it."

"I have to work Thursday and Friday. How about Saturday morning?"

"Done. I'll drive you home. I'm going to do some more hunting online, see what I can find out about Frederick Thornton and his partnership with Cornelius."

"Make sure to check the obituaries, you might find something there. And see if you can find anything more about Walter Merrick. Text me if you learn something."

That evening, when dinner was over, Simon asked Mrs. Morley about Edmund and Cornelius, hoping to learn more about them.

Mrs. Morley took a seat at the dining table, telling them how nice Edmund had been to her when she first came to Wilder House, promising that she would be treated fairly, kindly, and would earn a proper salary, confessing to her that as a boy he had witnessed all too often the harsh treatment of the household staff by Cornelius, and he had vowed never to treat his staff in a similar fashion.

Edmund had also told Mrs. Morley how ruthless Cornelius had been, both in business and in his personal life. No matter how much money he had, it was never enough, he still wanted more. Edmund had seen a dreadful gnawing emptiness inside his grandfather that could not be filled by money or power, in the same way that food eaten in a dream does not satiate hunger. Mrs. Morley was teary-eyed by the end of her story, saying what a wonderful man Edmund was, and to Simon's great embarrassment, how much Simon reminded her of Edmund.

After dinner Simon returned to his room, continuing his online search for information about Cornelius and his partner Frederick Thornton. He found a number of articles in the Caligo Falls Gazette archives about Edmund, most of them referencing his generous donations to the town, then found what he was looking for, a 1914 article about Cornelius and his partnership with Frederick Thornton.

*Caligo Falls Gazette, March 20, 1914*

***A Decade of Progress: The Legacy of Cornelius Wilder and Frederick Thornton***

*As we reflect on the past decade, the Midland &
Southern Railways emerges as a beacon of progress
and innovation. This year marks the tenth anniversary
of the partnership between Cornelius Wilder and
Frederick Thornton, two visionaries whose collaboration significantly impacted American rail travel.*

*In 1904, Wilder and Thornton joined forces to cre-
ate the Midland & Southern Railways, aiming to connect the Midwest with the South through a reliable
and efficient rail network. Their combined efforts led
to rapid expansion and economic growth in the regions their railway served.*

*Cornelius Wilder, known for his insight and lead-
ership, was instrumental in guiding the railway's development. In 1905, he built Wilder House in Caligo
Falls, a grand summer residence that quickly became
a local symbol of prosperity and progress.*

*Frederick Thornton, with his technical expertise
and engineering skills, complemented Wilder's vision
perfectly. His commitment to excellence ensured that
the Midland & Southern Railways set new standards
for safety and reliability in the industry.*

*Their partnership flourished, resulting in a decade
of success and growth. However, this year marks a
new chapter as the partnership is amicably dissolved.*

*Thornton is leaving to establish the Grand Union Railway Line, while the Midland & Southern Railways will continue to thrive under Wilder's leadership.*

*Despite the end of their formal partnership, the two men will continue to collaborate, sharing routes and working in tandem to maintain seamless connectivity for passengers.*

*Reflecting on their journey, Cornelius Wilder stated, "The past ten years have been incredibly rewarding. Frederick Thornton's contributions have been invaluable, and our collaboration has laid a strong foundation for the future."*

Simon read the article three times, growing more dubious each time he read through it. The journalist's glowing description of Cornelius and his close friendship with Thornton did not sound anything like the stories told to him by Harrington or Mrs. Morley. It sounded more like a public relations piece than authentic journalism.

There was another question that kept nagging at him: was it significant that Thornton was murdered in Caligo Falls? Did it implicate Cornelius in any way, or was it just a coincidence?

Simon continued searching the archives, his focus turning to Walter Merrick, curious about what had become of the man who murdered Josiah Finch. There was only one article, a story from 1924 about Police Chief Merrick retiring and moving to sunny California to take advantage of the region's famously temperate climate. It went on to say that Cornelius Wilder had purchased a small bungalow for Merrick on the southern California coastline, a benevolent display of his appreciation for Chief Merrick's long and distinguished service to Caligo Falls.

Simon leaned back in his chair with a sigh, closing his laptop. He knew Cornelius was not the kind of person who made benevolent gestures, like buying someone a home out of the kindness of his heart. There had to be a very good reason why he bought Merrick a house, possibly a bribe to keep him quiet about Thornton and Finch's murders. One thing Simon knew for certain, they were not going to learn the unvarnished truth about Cornelius, Thornton, and Merrick by reading old newspaper articles.

# Chapter 13

Simon was helping his mom do laundry when his phone beeped. It was a text from Clara.

*Any luck with the Thornton and Merrick search?*

*Merrick retired in 1924 and moved to southern California. It said Cornelius bought him a house to thank him for his service to Caligo Falls.*

*Mmm....that sounds highly unlikely.*

*I know. I found another article saying Cornelius and Thornton amicably dissolved their partnership in 1914, that Thornton started his own rail line.*

*Amicably? Really?*

*We're not going to learn the truth from old newspaper articles.*

*See if you can find out anything about the two guys who bought Merrick's police car. If we find the car, maybe we find Thornton's ghost.*

*Good idea — I'm on it!*

Simon took his laptop to the second floor sitting area, beginning his search for the two people who had purchased the 1917 police car: C.Whitaker and D.River. Frederick Thornton had been murdered in Merrick's patrol car, shot three times through the windshield, so it was possible that finding the car might lead them to Thornton's ghost.

Despite almost an hour of searching, he found nothing, no mention of a C.Whitaker or D.River. It did not come as a complete shock to Simon, well aware that the sale of a used car in 1926 was not exactly a newsworthy event.

"It's probably a big pile of rust, long gone."

He closed his eyes, wondering what a ghost like Frederick Thornton would do if the car he was psychically connected to rusted away to nothingness. Where would he go? Would he even know the car was gone? Would he be looking at a ghost car? And what kind of ghost would Thornton be? Was he like the ghosts of Edward Briggs and Asterius, chained to one spot, unaware of the passage of time? Or was he like Robert Sawyer, traipsing across the world, a spectral tourist? Or like Darlene Morley, living in a fog, unaware even that she had died.

He shut off his laptop, grabbing his phone and texting Clara.

*I can't find anything about the guys who bought the police car.*

*It was a long shot. I have Mom's car — I'll come over after work and we can check out the fourth closet. It must be important, but it might not have anything to do with the murders.*

*I hope it's not creepy like the ghost of Edward Briggs.*

*I'm guessing ten killer ghosts with ghost axes.*

*Ha ha.*

Clara arrived at 4:30, Simon waiting for her on the porch. She climbed out of the car, holding up a small brown paper bag.

"What's that?"

"A treat, a giant cinnamon roll. We can share it."

"Thanks. If we get murdered by ghosts, at least we won't be hungry."

"I thought you were the physics guy? How is a ghost

going to murder you? They don't exist in the physical world."

"All true, of course, but they could scare me to death, wave their arms and moan, clanking big chains and stuff."

"If you survived the ghost of Edward Briggs, you can survive anything."

"True again. He was totally terrifying."

They ate the cinnamon roll on their way down to the basement, Simon taking the ghost ring from his pocket as they approached the fourth door. He stopped, looking around.

"I think Frankie is here. I don't get a chill from him anymore, but I can kind of sense his presence."

"I think you're right, I'm getting a ghosty feeling."

"A ghosty feeling? That's probably not something a professional paranormal investigator should say."

"Put the ring on."

Clara took Simon's hand as he slipped on the ring, the ghost of Frankie Doyle appearing, toy horse in hand. He darted behind Simon, peering up at Clara.

Clara kneeled down, smiling, her eyes on Frankie.

"Hi, Frankie. You met me at the cemetery, remember? We brought flowers for your mom. Simon has told me so much about you, how nice you are and how much he likes you. He said he's glad to have a friend like you in this big old house."

Frankie inched forward, looking up at Simon.

Simon nodded. "Clara's right, it is nice to have you for a friend. You don't need to be shy around Clara, she's your friend too."

Clara pointed to the fourth door. "Frankie, we're going into that closet to see what's in there. Have you ever been in there?"

"The smoke hurt my nose."

Simon's eyes widened. "Smoke?"

"It hurt my nose. I don't like it."

Frankie vanished, Simon's face transformed into a mask of concern. "Why would there be smoke? What kind of smoke? That doesn't sound good at all."

"Only one way to find out." Clara pulled on the rope, the door sliding open, an extraordinary sight revealed to the two friends, Simon's jaw dropping.

Clara studied the opulent Victorian sitting room, lavishly furnished with highly polished mahogany furniture, brightly burning Tiffany gas lamps, two ornate couches, and several colorful antique vases holding freshly cut flowers. Three comfortable stuffed armchairs were facing a cozy fireplace, a pair of carved stone lions sitting on either side of the hearth.

Two men and one woman were seated in the armchairs. The men were wearing clothes from different eras, one from the early nineteen hundreds, and one from the eighteen hundreds. The man from the 1800s was puffing on a large ivory pipe. The woman was dressed in more modern clothes, possibly from the 1930s.

One of the men turned his head, setting his glass of wine down on a small round table next to him.

"Great heavens, we have visitors!"

The two others turned, studying Simon and Clara. "Are they deceased?"

"They don't appear to be."

"They must be friends of Edmund. They can see us?"

"Indeed, the boy is wearing Edmund's Shadow Ring, that would explain it."

"He wasn't wearing the ring when he previously visited us."

"You are quite correct in that. He was most certainly not wearing it then. I would have remembered such an event as that."

"Rather a lovely young lady, don't you think? I believe she is Emma, Edmund's true love. She bears an uncanny resemblance to Edmund's portraits of her. Would she still be alive?"

Simon raised one hand. "We can hear you?"

"Ah, of course you can, the ring, I do apologize. Are you a painter, an artiste? You bear a rather striking resemblance to Edmund Wilder. Might you be his son?"

The man smoking the pipe shook his head. "Less than a negligible chance of that, sir. Edmund was born in 1925. Perhaps this young man is his grandson."

"Also quite impossible, as Edmund and Emma never had any children of their own."

"You are quite correct. This is indeed a conundrum. Perhaps a distant cousin visiting from a faraway land?"

The woman raised one eyebrow. "Perhaps a visitor from Plindor?"

The two men laughed uproariously, one of them almost spilling his glass of wine.

"Such a marvelous witticism, indeed!"

"And one which could spring only from the agile mind of Agnes Victoria Holloway, renowned literary genius."

Simon looked at Clara, noting her baffled expression, then looked back at the curious residents of this very unusual room.

"Hi, my name is Simon Moody, Edmund Wilder's great nephew. He left the ghost ring to me in his will. My mom and I live here in Wilder House now. This is Clara Barley, the granddaughter of Emma Weatherby. Edmund gave me the key to this room and a cryptic note."

"You are an artiste, following in the footsteps of your illustrious uncle? You are here to paint for us?"

"No, I'm not an artist, I'm going to college this fall

and plan on majoring in physics. Clara is going to major in psychology."

The pipe smoking man gave the others a sideways glance. "Does anyone else feel as though they were reading yesterday's newspaper?"

More laughter, one of the men slapping his leg. "Very clever indeed, yesterday's newspaper. Quite droll."

Simon's eyes narrowed. The ghosts were beginning to annoy him. "Why is that funny?"

"We know all about you and Kate and Clara and Mrs. Morley and Harrington and Marion Jaggers and Darlene and Edward Briggs and Asterius and–"

Simon held up one hand. "Stop, I get it, you know everything that happens in the house."

"And a great number of other houses."

More laughter, the 1800s ghost madly puffing on his pipe, a cloud of blue swirling smoke obscuring his head.

Simon absently wondered if smoking would be bad for a ghost. One thing was for certain, his pipe was definitely the source of the smoke Frankie had mentioned.

Clara gave a bright smile. "You were all friends with Edmund?"

"Oh, yes indeed, the very best of friends, such a lovely man he was."

"Who are you, exactly?"

The 1900s ghost waved one hand theatrically, his

voice booming across the room. "We are the magnificent LOST, at your service."

"You're lost?"

Once again, the three ghosts roared with laughter. "Befuddles them every time, does it not?"

"Indeed it does, sir."

The man in the 1900s suit stood up, taking a deep bow. "I am Roland Barnsworth, professor emeritus at the Massachusetts Institute of Technology, an esteemed member of the physics department at that noble institution for almost forty years."

Simon blinked. "That's where I'm going to college in the fall. You used to teach there?"

"Quite so, for almost forty years."

"I'm confused, why are you here in Wilder House? Did you all die here?"

The professor turned to the others. "Shall we let them in on our little secret?"

"Of course, he is Edmund's great nephew, it is his birthright to know. Perhaps he will paint for us, just as Edmund did."

"Asked and answered, sir. He has already told us he is not an artiste, his interests lie only in the physical laws of this world."

The woman from the 1930s added, "And the young lady is Emma's lovely granddaughter. She also has a

162

right to know."

"Very well, the vote is unanimous. I can now tell you that LOST is an acronym, not a word."

"An acronym for what?"

"It is an acronym for the League of Spectral Tourists."

Simon glanced at Clara.

Clara said, "Spectral tourists? Like Robert Sawyer? You visit places like the Eiffel Tower and the Great Pyramid of Giza?"

"Robert Sawyer, you say? Was he not the poor fellow who was murdered by his dreadfully greedy wife? Aconitine, was it not? A ghastly affair, to be sure."

Simon nodded. "That's him, he's been visiting all the sights in Europe that he never got to see, like the Eiffel Tower."

The pipe smoking ghost gave an amused smile. "Not to be impertinent, but the good Dr. Sawyer is not exactly in our league, is he?"

The others laughed. "A brilliant play on words, sir, your clever utilization of the word *league*. I believe you missed your calling, you would have made a marvelous writer, perhaps penning a series of satirical novels?"

Simon eyed the three ghosts. "I'm very confused. You're saying Robert Sawyer is not a member of your League of Spectral Tourists?"

The professor gave Simon a sympathetic look. "It is

time for you to peruse more fully the collection of Edmund Wilder's paintings that rest on the shelves before you, scrutinizing each painting with razor sharp focus and single-minded intensity. Such a studious examination shall clarify the true nature of the League of Spectral Tourists."

"I looked at one of the paintings already. Wasn't Edmund just experimenting with a different style of painting, trying different color palettes?"

The professor motioned Simon and Clara toward the rack of paintings. "It has been said that a picture is worth a thousand words, but in this particular case, a picture is worth infinitely more."

The woman nodded. "Well said, sir."

Simon and Clara stepped toward the rack of paintings, Simon stopping to pass his hand through the back of an ornate couch. "My hand goes right through it."

"Precisely, the furniture before you is not of the physical world, being quite similar to the objects found in your dreams, created in much the same manner."

The writer, Agnes Victoria Holloway, added, "Each month we create a new motif for the room, varying the ambiance, the theme often based on designs we have seen in…" She hesitated, glancing expectantly at the other members of LOST.

The professor rubbed his chin. "Perhaps it would be

best to let them peruse the paintings first?"

Simon pulled out one of the canvases, studying it, tilting his head, squinting one eye. "Is that a giant insect?"

"Look closer, tell me what else you see."

"It's wearing a metal helmet and carrying a spear?"

"And in the sky?"

"Some kind of strange flying machines."

"Excellent, try the next one."

Clara pulled one out, eyeing it curiously. "A big yellow octopus in a desert, standing in front of some kind of multi-wheeled pirate ship with three masts and big sails. There are octopuses standing on the deck of the ship. They're wearing clothes, and hats. One has a sword."

Simon said, "Edmund illustrated science fiction book covers?"

"He did not, my young friend."

"So he just made this stuff up? It's kind of cool, really different from all his other art."

"A logical assumption, but also an incorrect one. Try again, sir."

Simon pulled out a painting of three Roman legionnaires wearing armor, each of their silver helmets topped with a red horsehair crest. The soldiers were standing next to what looked like a high tech alien space ship sitting in a lush meadow covered with long waving purple grass. "This is making no sense at all."

Clara called out, "Undersea snake creatures driving a silver and glass tracked vehicle along the ocean floor. I don't recognize any of the fish, if that's what they are. Some are carrying weapons, they look kind of like squids."

"Edmund didn't just make this up?"

"He did not."

Clara snapped her fingers, spinning around to face the three ghosts. "You're space tourists, you traveled to other worlds and told Edmund what you saw. These are paintings he did of the alien worlds you visited."

All three ghosts clapped in unison, the 1800s man whistling and cheering. "Well done, miss. Well done, indeed."

"The secret is out, the horse has left the barn. The acronym LOST serves a dual purpose, also being an acronym for Legion of Space Travelers."

Simon's mouth was hanging open. "You're serious? You saw all this on other worlds? How is that possible? These planets must be thousands of light years away, there's no way you could travel that far. Nothing can travel faster than the speed of light."

The professor laughed. "And therein lies the solution, young man. *Nothing* can travel faster than the speed of light."

"I just said that."

"And you were correct."

Simon was beginning to think the physics professor was missing a few nuts and bolts. "If nothing can travel faster than the speed of light, how could you travel there and back?"

The woman held up one hand. "Professor, there is no need to torment the boy any longer. After all, he is Edmund's great nephew."

# Chapter 14

"Very well. Simon Moody, I pose to you the following questions: I am a ghost, but what exactly is a ghost? When the physical body dies, what is it that continues on?"

"Some kind of conscious energy field?"

"There is no form of energy whatsoever capable of traveling faster than the speed of light. You know this."

"So what are you? What is a ghost?"

"A true ghost is pure universal consciousness without physical form. Consciousness is not energy, it is not physical matter, it is something else entirely, something existing outside of your physical and temporal dimensions, and yet, it is something which permeates every atom and molecule in your universe. It exists, but it doesn't exist. It is quantumly entangled with the human form, or a rabbit form, or a dog, or a huge yellow Plindorian octopus, or a small rock lying on the floor of a barren alien desert.

"It is somewhat of a misnomer to say that ghosts can travel faster than light. There is a self-perception that we are traveling from one point to another in the universe, which is subjectively true, but objectively false. We are not traveling in the sense of moving an object from one point to another, but we are merely changing the center of our awareness from one point to another within the field of universal consciousness. Again, this can be subjectively perceived as traveling instantly to another world, but such is not the case. You are here, but you are also there, connected to all things, you are everywhere, but you can relocate your center point of awareness to be anywhere within the realm of universal consciousness.

Simon stared at the professor. "How could something be nothing? That makes no sense."

"Let us try a different tack. I will pose three additional questions. You are having a dream, and in that dream you find yourself scaling a rugged, treacherous peak in Alaska with a team of fellow climbers. The first question is, how does that magnificent snowcapped mountain fit inside your head?"

"The mountain isn't real, it's just a dream, a thought in your head. Real mountains are real, not just a thought."

"The second question is, who were you in the dream?"

"You just said I was the guy climbing the mountain."

The professor smiled, glancing at the others. "The

third question is, if you were the mountain climber, then who were the other climbers, who was the mountain, who was the snow, who was the sky?"

Simon stared at the professor, his brow furrowed. "What?"

The woman frowned, shaking her head.

The man from the 1800s peered over his small gold spectacles at the professor. "You know quite well it is impossible for young Simon to understand such concepts while he is entangled with his physical earthly form. It is like trying to explain color to a blind man, music to a deaf man. Such things must be experienced to be understood. You are well aware of this."

The doctor rubbed his chin, nodding. "You are quite correct, sir. At times, I forget what life was like when I too was entangled with a physical form. Simon, you should know that Edmund understandably also found the science of consciousness to be quite unfathomable. That being said, he was wise enough to realize it didn't really matter. The important thing for him was to experience the wonders of this world in the time that he had, much as an undersea diver has a limited time to search for treasure on the ocean floor."

Simon was silent for a moment, then said. "I know I don't understand this, but whatever it is, it's science, and one day they will be teaching it in schools. Anything that

170

exists is based in science, whatever, wherever, whenever, or whoever it is."

The professor smiled. "Excellent, you would have made a marvelous student. Perhaps you shall be the first professor at the Massachusetts Institute of Technology to teach a class on the physics of consciousness."

Clara said, "Could I ask a question, one not about physics?"

The writer smiled. "Of course you may."

"Do you know anything about the murder of Cornelius Wilder's partner, Frederick J. Thornton? We're trying to find out who really killed him. We know that Josiah Finch was framed for the murder by Police Chief Walter Merrick in 1923, that Josiah was not the one who killed Thornton."

The 1800s man rose up from his chair. "Forgive my rudeness for not previously introducing myself. I am Dr. Benjamin Aldridge, a retired surgeon, born 1819, died 1883. I roamed the Earth for many years before hearing rumors of a group calling themselves the League of Spectral Tourists, brave stalwart spirits traveling to far distant realms. It was not until the year 1963 that Edmund and his Shadow Ring became known to us. It was his idea to paint what we had seen on those other worlds. He would touch one of us, reliving our memories of a particular world, seeing it with his own eyes. Then he would paint it, a permanent record of the fantastical sights we had witnessed.

"I was present in 1918 when the pandemic arrived in Caligo Falls. Within several weeks many of the household staff had perished, the cemetery in the woods crowded with the spirits of those poor souls, most of them confused, disoriented. Medicine in 1918 had advanced far beyond what it was in my day, but viruses were still a deadly mystery. We did what we could to help the victims move on, some taking more time than others. Poor Frankie Doyle never moved on, waiting here patiently for his mother. Nothing we said or did would change his mind. I am glad to see he has found new friends in you and Clara. Perhaps you shall be the ones to help him find his way home."

Clara said, "Um, about the murder of Frederick Thornton?"

"Drat, I've done it again, haven't I? I do tend to veer off the tracks on occasion. To answer your original question, I have no knowledge of Frederick Thornton's murder, but I do know he and Cornelius Wilder became bitter rivals after the dissolution of their partnership. Sometimes I would hear them having the most dreadful arguments on the telephone, using language that would make a sailor blush."

Simon turned to Agnes, saying, "Are there any other

ghosts living in Wilder House that we don't know about? We know about Frankie, but we're trying to locate Walter Merrick, Frederick Thornton, and Tobias Granger. "

"There are none in Wilder House besides young Frankie, I'm afraid, but there are two others I am aware of on the Wilder estate."

"Where are they?"

"For reasons I am unable to divulge at this time, I shall only mention one, and I hesitate to do even that. That being said, there is an unmarked grave hidden behind the small cemetery in the woods. The spirit who resides there is not one you would wish to encounter. It is a dark hearted being, angry beyond measure, filled with the most vile and obsessive thoughts of revenge."

"Revenge against who?"

"The details of his dire circumstances are unknown to us. There is no communication with this being, it is confined within itself, a Gordian Knot of sorts, lost to the world, existing in a nightmarish prison of its own creation. I have only seen one or two others like this. A dark spirit such as this one is rare, but they do exist, and it is best to stay far away from them."

Simon frowned. "That sounds a lot like Edward Briggs."

Dr. Aldridge shook his head. "This spirit is far worse than poor Edward Briggs ever was, far darker. Edward

Briggs was ravaged by profound guilt, but this spirit is burning with an unbridled fiery rage."

Simon turned to Clara. "Not going to happen. No way."

She nodded. "Agreed, we stay away from it."

Simon asked, "How long has the League of Spectral Tourists existed?"

"Three or four hundred years at least, the league originating in Paris, members coming from all across the globe. As you might well imagine, we were most certainly not the first spirits to roam the universe, but perhaps we were the first organized league of spirits to do so. There are other leagues out there now, but we were the first."

A curious thought popped into Simon's head. "Do beings from other worlds roam the universe after they die? Do they visit Earth?"

"Indeed they do, but not as often as you might think. There are millions of civilizations to be found across the universe, but to put it delicately, this is not a popular destination. Earth is considered excessively primitive and brutally violent by most standards. There are beings out there who have evolved far beyond anything you might imagine."

"Like what?"

Dr. Aldridge turned to the others. "Perhaps a memory

of Sinaria would suffice?"

The professor looked dubious. "I don't know, one must be careful about such things, sir. There are rules."

"Pish posh, no one would believe him anyway, they would think his words to be the incoherent ravings of a madman."

"You make a valid point." The doctor looked at Simon and Clara. "Would you care to relive a memory in the same manner that Edmund did?"

"What kind of memory?"

"It is the memory of a world called Sinaria, a unique world I visited briefly over a hundred years ago."

"It's safe to do this, right?"

"Edmund relived many of our memories with no ill effects."

Clara said, "Simon, let's do it. How amazing would it be to visit another world?"

"It would be very amazing."

Simon took Clara's hand, stepping over to the doctor. "When you touch my hand the memory shall begin."

Simon reached out, touching the doctor's hand.

The room vanished, replaced by a seemingly endless sea of pale blue grass and colorful blossoms, gloriously tall yellow trees swaying in a warm breeze. Simon was getting a strange feeling that somehow the trees were aware of his presence. A series of sparkling glass towers appeared on the distant horizon, their presence filling Simon with a profound and overwhelming sense of joy.

"What is this place? Why do I feel like this?"

He heard Clara's voice. "Simon, I think the flowers are singing. Do you hear that?"

"I hear it. I think the trees are talking."

Dr. Aldridge's voice sounded. "This is Sinaria, a world of infinite mystery, even to the most advanced of civilizations."

"Who lives here?"

An otherworldly being appeared in front of them, a pure white creature with a bulbous head, no eyes, no ears, no face. It had long ropy arms and legs, the creature floating six inches above the blue grass.

"We see you have returned, Dr. Aldridge, bringing with you two friends. What is the purpose of your visit?"

"No, sir, that is quite impossible, this is only a memory, I am allowing them to relive my memory."

"Nevertheless, here you are with your new friends, Simon Moody and Clara Barley, standing in the world of Sinaria."

Simon went into panic mode. "This isn't a memory, we're actually here in Sinaria?"

The Sinarian glowed with a soft light. "It is very, very complicated. You are here, you are not here, it is a memory, it is not a memory, this is a world of nonduality. The truth of the matter is, you have no understanding of the interaction between reality and consciousness. You are stumbling through a dark forest, a small dim flashlight in your hand, trying to find your way. You are an ant gazing upward as an interstellar time walker blinks into a brilliant green sky, the ant attempting to make sense of what he is seeing. You must return to your world, that is where you are meant to be. One day you will understand, but that day is not today."

The Sinarian vanished, Simon and Clara finding themselves back in the fourth closet. Simon staggered backwards. "What was that? What happened?"

The doctor shook his head. "I am as mystified as you are."

"Were we really there, or was it your memory?"

"The Sinarian would have us believe it was both."

Simon groaned. "I think my head's going to explode."

"As I said, Sinaria is unique, a world unlike others, but you will be pleased to know that most worlds are similar in nature to Earth. They may be technologically far more advanced, but in all other respects they are quite similar."

The writer nodded. "And that is why there are only three of us left in LOST."

"What do you mean?"

"If you travel to enough worlds, you will discover that

like fingerprints, they are all different, but conversely, they are all the same. They are governed by the physical nature of the universe. The inhabitants have physical bodies that need nourishment, they get sick, they can be injured, killed. They are mobile, using legs or wings or fins or a myriad of other appendages to move from place to place. They reproduce, have young that need to be raised, they grow old, they are mortal, and though some may live artificially for many centuries, their physical bodies all eventually die. That is why Edmund gave you the quote that he did. *In one drop of water are found all the secrets of the oceans.*

"Universal consciousness permeates the universe, found within an infinite variety of physical life forms, but again, like fingerprints, they are essentially all the same. If you understand the nature of one life form, you understand the nature of all of them. The members of the league came to realize this, becoming bored, deciding they had seen all they needed to see here, that it was time to move on."

Clara glanced at her watch, giving a start. "Simon, we have to go, Mom needs her car back. I can't be late."

Simon nodded, his eyes on Dr. Aldridge's hand. "Are you glowing?"

"Indeed not, sir, you are quite mistaken. I fear the light is playing tricks on your eyes."

Agnes said, "It is the glow of the gas lamps, an illusion."

Simon nodded. "You're right, it's those flickering gas lamps."

"We have to go, Simon." Clara waved to the three ghosts. "Thank you so much for talking to us. Can we come back again and visit?"

"Of course you may. We shall be looking forward to your return."

Simon and Clara darted out of the room and up the back stairs. As they ran along the porch toward the parking area, Simon said, "The doctor was glowing, I'm sure of it."

"I know. He started to glow after he told you about the quote, what it meant."

"They don't want him to go."

"And he doesn't want to go."

# Chapter 15

Simon awoke the next morning, his thoughts returning to the three ghosts in the fourth closet. It was almost impossible to imagine a universe holding millions of civilizations across billions of light years. And the professor's talk about universal consciousness was mind boggling, impossible to understand. He liked what Edmund had said, that the important thing was to experience the wonders of the world while we are here. He could do that.

He got dressed and headed downstairs, finding his mom at the dining room table, drinking her morning coffee. She looked up at him, smiling. "Good morning, sweetie."

"Morning. Have you seen Harrington? I had a few questions I wanted to ask him about the history of Wilder House."

"He's not here, he had errands to run in Deep River. He should be back this afternoon."

Simon was stabbing his fork into a blueberry pancake when it hit him like the proverbial shooting star on a dark night. Harrington was in Deep River. Deep River. That was it, D.River was not the name of a person who bought the old police car, D.River was a place. The car was bought by someone named C.Whitaker in the township of Deep River, New Hampshire. This was a huge breakthrough, greatly narrowing their search for the car. C.Whitaker would have died years ago, but maybe one of his descendants still retained possession of the police car. He grabbed his phone to text Clara.

"No texting at the table."

"Sorry, I forgot."

"What are you up to today?"

"I don't know for sure, but Clara's off today so I was thinking we might drive to Deep River, see what it's like. I haven't really seen much of the area around here, mostly just Caligo Falls."

"That sounds nice. Harrington says it's a lovely town, quaint, picturesque, with lots of little farms. Maybe you could pick up some fresh veggies for Mrs. Morley while you're there."

"Right, fresh veggies for Mrs. Morley."

When breakfast was over, Simon went outside, taking a seat in a wicker chair on the porch, texting Clara.

*Who's a genius? This guy. D.River is a place, not a person – Deep River.*

*Brilliant! We can search online for people named Whitaker living in Deep River.*

*Exactly. Text me if you find something. I'll look too.*

*Did you find the safe yet?*

*Ha ha.*

Simon ran up to his room, grabbing his laptop.

"Okay, people named Whitaker in Deep River."

He frowned at the long list of names that appeared. There were a lot of people named Whitaker in Deep River. It must be an old family, been there forever, like the Finches in Caligo Falls. He scrolled slowly down the list, stopping abruptly when something caught his eye.

"Holy crap! This is it. This has to be it!"

**Billy Whitaker's Antique Car Museum**
**Open seven days a week, 9am – 7pm**
**Adults $10, small children Free**

His phone beeped seconds later.

*Did you see it?*

*Billy Whitaker's Antique Car Museum!!!!*

*We're going to Deep River. Bring your ring.*

*I'll be there in twenty minutes.*

Simon grabbed the ghost ring from his bedside table and ran downstairs, calling out to his mom. "I'm leaving! Clara and I are driving to Deep River."

"Don't forget fresh veggies for Mrs. Morley. She loves tomatoes."

"Right, fresh tomatoes. Bye!"

Simon darted down the hill to the carriage house, and ten minutes later was speeding down the narrow highway toward the Caligo Falls town center. Clara was waiting for him on the front porch of her house.

She hopped into the car, grabbing his arm. "I can't believe we may have located the old police car."

"If there's a ghost in it, which ghost would it be?"

"Either Frederick Thornton or Walter Merrick."

"Unless it's someone else, some unknown person who murdered Thornton."

"We can't get too excited, the car might not even be there."

Simon started the engine, the pair of friends heading north on the narrow winding highway.

"Not many houses out here. Lots of trees though."

Clara said, "Are you getting excited about college?"

"The summer is going by way too fast. I'm excited, but kind of scared too. Everyone there is going to be super smart."

"Then you'll fit right in."

"Thanks, but I didn't feel super smart when Professor Barnsworth was explaining universal consciousness. I felt like a six-year-old trying to understand quantum physics. And that crazy Sinarian, I had no idea what he was talking about."

"It's all relative. Besides, they said it would be impossible for us to understand consciousness and time while we're here in these physical bodies. Let it go, do fun stuff, enjoy life while we're here."

"I know, I just wish I knew what it all meant, how it all worked."

"Then you'd be happy?"

"I know what you're doing, and I'm happy right now, even without knowing all that. Driving through a beautiful forest on a sunny summer day with my best friend in the world next to me. What could be better than that?"

Clara moved closer to him. "Nothing could be better than that."

"Wait, you mean *nothing* is better than that? Like *nothing* can travel faster than the speed of light?"

Clara punched his arm. "Don't be an idiot."

"Marion said only lovebirds talk like that. Are we

lovebirds?"

"We are definitely lovebirds, Simon Moody."

"Just checking."

An hour later Simon pointed to a green highway sign. "There it is, Deep River, 10 miles. We're almost there."

Clara checked her phone. "I entered the museum address in GPS maps. We go through the town center, drive north five miles, then turn right on Dead Horse Road."

"I wonder why they call it Dead Horse Road? Kind of a weird place to have a car museum, out in the middle of nowhere."

"It's probably some guy who turned his huge car collection into a museum. That happens a lot."

"You're probably right." They passed through the town center, Simon glancing at the quaint New England style shops and homes. "This looks kind of like Caligo Falls. Oh, if we see a roadside veggie stand I'm supposed to get tomatoes for Mrs. Morley."

"We already passed three of them. We can stop on the way back."

"Nice. How much farther?"

"We turn right onto Dead Horse Road in three miles."

Simon slowed down five minutes later. "Should be around here somewhere. Look for a street sign."

"The GPS says we passed it."

"No way, I didn't see a road."

"Turn around, we have to go back. We definitely passed it."

Simon turned the truck around, driving slowly down the highway. "I'm not seeing anything."

"Stop!"

"What is it?"

"I think that's a road."

"It looks like an old hiking trail."

"Let's get out and take a look."

They pulled over and climbed out of the truck, stepping over to an eight-foot-wide dirt trail partially hidden by tall grass and weeds.

Clara pointed mutely to a decrepit hand painted wooden sign nailed to a tree.


### Dead Horse Road
### Car Museum 3 miles


Simon shook his head. "No way. Not happening. This is exactly how horror movies begin; a young couple driving down an old deserted road, stopping at a weird farmhouse to ask directions. A crusty old guy in coveralls steps out of a barn carrying a chainsaw."

Clara laughed. "And he says, 'You folks lost? Big storm last night, the bridge is washed out. You'll have to spend the night in the barn with the *others*.'"

Simon stared at Clara. "What are you doing?"

"Nothing."

"Fine, you got me, I watch too many scary movies. I know there's not going to be a scary guy with a chainsaw, I was just speculating."

"The road's not too bad, we'll be fine, put the truck in low gear. It will all be worth it if we find the police car."

"Okay, let's do this."

It took them twenty minutes to make their way down the bumpy, rutted, curving road, Simon stopping when he saw the old ramshackle farmhouse.

"I knew it, an old farmhouse, I told you. This does not look like a museum, it looks like a hundred-year-old junkyard. Look at all that stuff: rusty old tractors and trucks and weird farm machinery. How can he call this a car museum?"

"It has old cars?"

Simon shut off the engine, stepping out of the truck.

"I don't see anyone. That's kind of creepy."

"Try honking your horn."

He reached into the truck, pressing the horn. Two minutes later a man wearing worn coveralls stepped out of the forest, Simon's eyes were focused like white hot lasers on the red chainsaw the man was carrying.

"Don't say it, Simon."

"I'm not going to say anything. I'm not going to say

he's wearing coveralls and carrying a chainsaw."

The man waved to them, setting the chainsaw down on a stump.

"Sorry, didn't hear you folks come in. Cutting firewood for the winter. Gotta stay warm."

"We wanted to check out the old cars."

"You come to the right place then. Got about ten acres of them, all kinds. You looking for parts? You rebuild the old ones? Looking for anything special?"

Simon said, "We like the old antique cars, especially old police cars. Do you have anything like that? An old police car?"

The man took off his well-worn Red Sox baseball cap, scratching his head. "Old antique police cars, eh? I'll have to think on that one for a spell. Seems like I might, maybe one of my grandpa's old cars. He started collecting them back in the 1920s. Most of them are rusty, but collectors like'em, restore them and sell them for big money."

"What was your grandpa's name?"

"Carl Whitaker. He passed away when I was teenager. Nicest guy you'd ever want to meet. Taught me all about cars. "

"Nice. Are his cars all in one area?"

"They are. Walk down that way as far as the cars go. Should find a bunch of old ones there, most of them covered with tarps. The tarps are probably covered with moss, and the moss is probably covered with bugs, but feel free to pull the tarps off, take a look. Seems like I recall he had a police car in there somewhere. Ten bucks each should cover it."

Simon paid the man and they pushed through the tall grass and weeds, Simon swatting at the buzzing insects.

"Did you see the size of that bee?"

Clara took his hand. "Does this help make the scary bee go away?"

"I wasn't scared of it, I just didn't want to get stung." He grinned. "But it does help scary stuff go away. No way would I be looking for a haunted car without you here."

"I wouldn't be here either."

"Down that way, check out all the moss covered tarps. That has to be his grandpa's old car collection."

They approached the maze of covered cars, Simon stepping over to one of them, pressing one finger gingerly against the spongy layer of moss. "Eew. How do we know which one is the police car?"

"I think it's that one over there, the one with the sign that says *Police Chief Merrick's Creepy Old Haunted Murder Car.*"

Simon burst out laughing. "Good one. Wait, the police car had a flashing red light on the roof, right? Look for a tarp with a big bump on top."

"Unless the red light is missing."

"Good point, we should check them all."

After having checked over two dozen cars, lifting the tarps high enough to verify it wasn't the car they were looking for, Clara spotted one with a bulge on the roof. "That could be it."

Simon ran over to the car, lifting the tarp. "It's an old ambulance. Kind of cool though. I should buy it and restore it, drive around Caligo Falls in a big old white ambulance. It would be a cool ghost hunting car."

"People would wave you down at car accidents, want you to stop, then call the police if you didn't."

"True."

"Let's try that one, it has a bump on top."

Simon walked over to the car, studying it. "It's the right shape, a long flat roof like a touring car, not a sedan."

Clara raised the tarp slightly. "Spoked wheels, that's a good sign."

She raised it higher, Simon giving a yelp when he read the faded white lettering on the rear passenger door. "Caligo Falls Police Department! This is it!"

Clara dropped the tarp back down. "This is the ghost car we saw, the actual real car that Chief Merrick was actually driving. He was sitting in this car."

"We did it, we found it. It's right in front of us. How completely amazing is this?"

"You know what we have to do now."

"Put on the ring, pull off the tarp, scream and run away?"

"Maybe there won't be a ghost, it might just be a rusty old relic from 1917."

"I don't think that's how it works. We're supposed to be here."

"Put the ring on and help me pull the tarp off."

"I have a better idea, let's pull the tarp off first, walk back twenty feet, and then put the ring on."

"So we'll have a head start if it comes after us?"

"Maybe."

# Chapter 16

Simon stomped down the tall weeds at the front end of the car, swatting at the flurry of buzzing insects that took to the air.

"These bugs are crazy. Okay, you take that corner of the tarp and I'll take this one. On three, we pull it up and over the car."

Clara nodded, kicking the moss off the lower section of the tarp. "Ready."

"One, two, three!"

The two friends yanked the tarp up, dragging it over the top of the car.

They stepped back from the vehicle, Simon brushing chunks of moss off his clothes and out of his hair, his eyes on the rusty 1917 police car once driven by Walter Merrick.

"Check out the license plate. This is the car."

Clara walked slowly around the vehicle, running her hand across the wide curving rusted fender. "Three bullet holes in the windshield."

Simon reached for the handle of the passenger door,

pulling on it, the door squealing painfully open. "Needs a little oil." He pointed to the cracked and worn leather seat. "Three holes in the back of the seat, and some kind of dark stain. Pretty sure I know what that is."

"It's the final proof that Frederick Thornton was murdered in this car. The murderer was standing in front of it and fired three times through the windshield, killing him."

"But the murderer wasn't Josiah Finch."

"It was definitely not him. I still can't believe we're standing next to the real ghost car."

Simon peered into the car's interior. "The back seat is empty. Anything Thornton had with him, like luggage or papers, is long gone. The police probably took it all. It might be in an evidence locker somewhere."

Clara circled back around to the passenger side of the car. "I hate to tell you this, paranormal investigative partner, but someone is here, in the car. I can feel it."

"Let's move back a little."

They stepped away from the car, Clara taking Simon's hand.

"Here goes nothing." Simon slipped the ring on, the color draining from his face.

The man in the passenger seat was looking in their direction, his white shirt and jacket soaked in blood, three holes in his shirt, his bloody hands pressing against

193

his wounds.

Simon lurched backwards when he heard the voice.

"I've been shot! Call for an ambulance, I'm bleed-ing!"

"He's a sleeper, he doesn't know he's dead."

Clara called out, "Are you Frederick J. Thornton?"

"I need help, I've been shot! Hurry!"

"How long have you been here?"

"I'm bleeding! Get me a doctor!"

"He's like Darlene, he has no idea how much time has passed since he died."

"He can't tell us anything, I don't think he hears us. He might not even see us."

"We have to relive his memories. If we can wake him, we can ask him questions."

"I guess we don't have a choice. Let's get this over with." Simon stepped closer to the open passenger door, eyeing the man's blood soaked shirt. He reached out and took Clara's hand. "Ready?"

Clara hesitated for a second, then touched Frederick Thornton's arm.

The junkyard vanished, Simon finding himself in a luxurious restaurant, several dozen men dressed in ele-gant formal attire seated around an immense polished dining table. Judging from the style of clothes and the lavishness of the table settings, Simon guessed this was a memory from the early 1900s, the Gilded Age. Many of the men were smoking cigars, drinking brandy.

A line of waiters wearing shiny black vests and silk bow ties marched into the room, each carrying a silver tray covered with a dome shaped lid.

"Clara, are you seeing this?"

"I'm here. I'm wearing a tuxedo. This has to be a memory of old New York, probably in Manhattan."

"It's definitely a luxury hotel."

A shrill whistle blew, the waiters moving as one, each setting a silver tray in front of a diner. When the whistle blew again, they removed the silver lids and stepped back, marching out of the room in unison at the sound of the third whistle.

"Yum, that smells good. Steak and potatoes, and some kind of veggie. Is that wine?"

"I think it's sherry, they used to have that a lot with dinners."

"How do you know about that?"

"I read a lot?"

Simon watched Thornton's arm reach out, picking up the glass of sherry, downing it in one gulp. He reached out for a small silver bell, ringing it, a waiter appearing fifteen seconds later.

"May I help you, sir?"

"Whiskey. Leave the bottle."

"Of course, sir."

Simon whispered. "This guy likes to drink."

Clara said, "Frederick, my name is Clara Barley. We found you in the police car, you'd been shot. We're reliving one of your memories. Can you hear me?"

"Who is that? Where are you?"

"We're reliving one of your memories from long ago. Do you recognize this place?"

"Of course I do, it's the Hotel Astor on Broadway in 1904. Cornelius is announcing our partnership, announcing the formation of Midland & Southern Railway."

"Who are these people? Were they friends of yours?"

"Business acquaintances, a mix of old money and new money. Most are old money, on Mary Astor's list of the 400. We were not on the 400, we were new money, looked down on by the arrogant bastards who call themselves old New York."

The man sitting next to Frederick stood up, tapping his glass with a silver spoon.

Simon looked at the man, giving a start. "Clara, it's Cornelius! We're sitting next to him."

Cornelius Wilder's voice boomed out across the lavishly appointed dining room.

"Gentlemen, forgive the interruption, but before dinner is served, I should like to make a brief but salient announcement."

Several of the diners groaned, murmuring among themselves, Simon could hear muffled laughter.

Cornelius continued. "I stand before you today to announce a new and irrefutably profitable collaboration between myself and Mister Frederick J. Thornton, one which promises to shape the future of American rail travel. Together, we shall embark on a new and ambitious endeavor, the creation of a modern rail line, Midland & Southern Railways, a shining beacon of progress and innovation.

"Our vision is clear, to connect the Midwest with the South through a reliable and efficient rail network. This partnership brings together two vital, ambitious, successful men, a partnership which will utilize my leadership and insight, and Frederick Thornton's unparalleled technical expertise and engineering skills. Our railway shall forge new standards for safety and reliability, driving the rapid expansion and economic growth of the regions we serve.

"Frederick Thornton's commitment to excellence will ensure that the Midland & Southern Railways becomes a model for the industry, his dedication to safety and reliability the cornerstone of our operations, guaranteeing our passengers and freight shall reach their destinations swiftly and securely.

"I pledge to guide this new enterprise with a steadfast

commitment to our shared vision. Together, Frederick and I shall forge a future where towns and cities flourish along our tracks, where industries thrive, and where communities are connected as never before. The Midland & Southern Railways will be more than just a transportation network; it will be a lifeline for progress and prosperity.

"We hope you will join us in this monumental endeavor, participating in the transformative impact the Midland & Southern Railways shall have on our great nation."

There was a smattering of applause, then the sound of forks and knives, clinking glasses, murmured conversation.

Cornelius took a seat, leaning over to Frederick, whispering to him. "Puffed up bastards, all of them, clinging with sad desperation to their dusty fortunes, fossils of a bygone era. I will crush them into the ground like the filthy little insects that they are."

Frederick laughed. "But not before emptying their wallets."

Cornelius gave a humorless smile. "We shall lay waste to them all."

The dining room vanished, Simon finding himself seated at an ornately carved wooden desk in a private luxury railcar, the car rhythmically swaying back and forth as it rolled down the tracks. A pale bespectacled man wearing a black suit and tie, his hair slicked back, was standing in front of the desk, his hands clasped together.

Simon whispered, "Clara, check out this train car. Super fancy, everything is velvet and brass and leather. It even has electric lights."

Clara said, "Why am I feeling so much anger, rage? Something bad is happening here."

Simon looked down at Thornton's hands, at the newspaper he was holding, the article he was reading, his knuckles white. There were two photographs, the first one of a lovely young woman standing on a stage holding a bouquet of flowers, the second was an unflattering photograph of Frederick Thornton. He slammed his fist down on the desk, roaring at the man in front of him. "How could this happen? Who did this? I will murder them, eviscerate them!"

The man in the black suit said, "I have reason to believe that one of Cornelius' men leaked the story to the newspaper. He is attempting to discredit you in the eyes of the stockholders."

"What did Cornelius say? Did he deny it?"

"He pleaded ignorance, of course, but the man who leaked it to the Tribune told me Cornelius had ordered him to do so. I paid the man quite handsomely for this information, and he had nothing to gain from lying."

Clara could feel the rage burbling through Frederick, his body shaking. "I know his secrets, the lies, the bribery, corruption, his underhanded schemes, and the women. I shall repay his treachery a thousandfold, filling the papers with his vile secrets. Midland & Southern will be mine, Wilder will be ruined."

"Sir, there's more, something far more serious than the newspaper article."

"What could be worse than that? Speak up, man!"

The man reached into his jacket pocket, pulling out a sheath of papers, setting them down on Thornton's desk, taking a step back, his hands once again clasped together.

Thornton studied the papers for almost a full minute, reading through the columns of numbers, then leaped to his feet. "This is a lie, it cannot be! He would not do this!"

"It is quite true, sir, Cornelius now owns sixty-seven percent of the Midland & Southern stock. I have spoken with our financiers and attorneys at great length."

"We were equal partners, how could this happen?"

"We believe Cornelius has been purchasing shares using phantom investors, men purporting to be buying shares for themselves, but in truth they were purchasing them for Cornelius, at his bequest. Over the last two years he has been amassing shares, slowly seizing control of the company. He has told the attorneys in confidence that he wishes to call a shareholder meeting for the purpose of voting you out of the company. I am certain the vote will succeed, considering the number of shares he holds and this recently published scandalous article regarding you and the young actress. There have been murmurs of possible criminal action in regards to this dalliance, but with a few payments to the right judges, nothing shall come of it. The public has a short memory for such salacious matters."

Thornton sat silently, his fists clenched, then looked up at the man in the black suit. His voice was low and dark and gravelly. "I will destroy him ten times over. I will obliterate everything he holds dear. I will sing my heart out to the newspapers."

"A pleasant notion indeed, sir, but I am uncertain whether the public holds trust in you at this time, and will perceive your actions as nothing more than a fabricated retaliatory act of revenge. Perhaps we might try a different tack."

"What are you suggesting?"

"You have many friends in the industry, and Cornelius is a highly unlikable character, despised by many, to say the least. Take your leave of Midland & Southern and start your own rail line, tell Cornelius it would be good for business to cooperate with each other, share the lines and the profits, a profitable collaboration, the two rail lines working in tandem."

"Why would I do such a thing?"

"As has often been said, revenge is a dish best served cold. When the time is right, when he is least expecting it, that is when we shall strike a crushing blow, grinding him into the dirt."

Thornton leaned back in his chair, drumming his stubby manicured fingers on the desktop. "Perhaps there is some merit to this plan. I like it. We shall need to discuss the necessary finances, find partners, investors, just as we did for Midland & Southern. Send a wire to Cornelius, tell him I am stepping down from the company, that I bear him no ill will, it was simply a business matter, nothing more, nothing less. Make no mention of my plans to form another rail line."

Simon said, "I knew there was more to this. The newspaper said the dissolution of their partnership had been amicable, that they were still friends. They got that part wrong."

"Dr. Aldridge was right when he told us Cornelius and Frederick had become bitter enemies."

"So who murdered Frederick Thornton, and why?"

"Maybe the young actress, the girl from the newspaper article?"

"Or someone close to her who was looking for

revenge."

The private train car faded to black, Simon and Clara finding themselves drifting in infinite darkness.

Clara called out, "Frederick, we need to relive the memory of your murder, we need to know who shot you when you were in the car with Police Chief Walter Merrick."

"I am not murdered, I am alive, but I need help, a doctor."

"Show us what you remember, what led up to the shooting, what you saw."

There was a blink of light, Simon and Clara facing a floor-to-ceiling window in a towering skyscraper, gazing down at the sprawling cityscape of old New York.

# Chapter 17

Simon gazed out across the city. "No Empire State Building, no Chrysler Building. We're looking at New York City in the early 1900s. I wish I had a camera."

"The newspaper article said they dissolved their partnership in 1914, Frederick starting his own railway, the Grand Union Railway Line."

Frederick pressed one hand against the window, a dark expression filling his face. "It's time we brought an end to that snake Cornelius Wilder." He turned to face the man behind him, the same man Simon and Clara had seen in the private rail car.

The man shrugged. "There is no doubt that he stole the contract from you, bribed our two favorite senators and the operations manager at Titan Oil. He stole it right out from under us."

"It's time to move, time to strike."

"I received a wire from him this morning. Cornelius has cordially invited you to visit him at his summer home in Caligo Falls, New Hampshire. He mentioned a mutually beneficial and highly lucrative shipping agreement."

"I have long since grown weary of his lies and empty promises. I shall go to the newspapers, tell them everything, name names, even the senators, the congressmen. We have documentation for all of it. It will be the biggest scandal to hit the newspapers since the Whiskey Ring. They will bury him."

"Perhaps you should meet with him first, listen to his proposition, use this information as leverage to get the oil contract back."

"Let cooler heads prevail? I suppose there is no real rush to this. It will be amusing to hear what foul lies spew from his mouth, all the while making my plans to destroy him."

"I shall make travel arrangements. You can take the train to Caligo Falls on Friday, return a day or two later."

"Why would anyone choose to live in such an ungodly place as that?"

The man in the black coat shrugged. "To each his own."

New York vanished, Simon and Clara drifting in the familiar black void.

"We're getting close. He's going to Caligo Falls to meet with Cornelius."

"Maybe the man in the black coat is a traitor, maybe he's working for Cornelius. Maybe he and Cornelius planned Frederick's murder."

The blackness vanished, replaced with a swaying train car holding several dozen passengers, pine forests rushing past on either side of the rumbling train.

Simon said, "We're on our way to Caligo Falls."

Clara called out, "Frederick, do you remember anything about your meeting with Cornelius in Caligo Falls, what he told you?"

Before they realized what was happening, Simon and Clara found themselves sitting in the dining room at Wilder House, Cornelius Wilder across the table from them, puffing on a cigar.

"What do you think of my proposition? It would be highly beneficial to both of us, worth many hundreds of thousands a year, possibly a great deal more."

"What do I think? I think I need another drink." Frederick reached for a bottle of whiskey on the table, filling his glass. He downed the glass, then clumsily set it down.

Simon said, "Why would he drink that stuff? It tastes like gasoline."

Frederick's speech was becoming slurred. "I want my oil contract back. You're a snake, you stole it from me, bribed the senators."

"Merely business, nothing more. This new proposition will make us millions, the oil shipping contract pales in comparison."

"I want it back. You're rich as Croesus but you always

want more, more, more. You're not shipping the oil, it's mine."

"The first rule is that money is power, surely you know this. And the second rule, you can never have enough of either."

Frederick poured another glass of whiskey, drinking it, dropping the glass on the table.

Cornelius studied Frederick's face. "Perhaps we should have some dinner, take a respite from the whiskey bottle."

"I will ruin you, crush you, grind you into the dirt. I want my contract back."

"I fear the whiskey has taken control of you. I will ring for dinner."

"I know about the girl, that much beloved sweet little songstress, shining young star of stage and silver screen. I have pictures, and I can tell you they weren't cheap. I want my oil contract or the pictures will be splashed across the front page of every newspaper in the country."

"Come now, Frederick, there's no need for threats. We all have our little secrets, and that includes you, old friend, in case you have forgotten."

"It's all documented, photos, signed contracts, your lies, the bribes, the two senators, the congressmen. I'll sing like a drunken sailor and the world will listen."

"Very well, you have successfully swayed my

decision. I will see what I can do about transferring the oil contract back to you. Are you still interested in my new proposition? We'll make millions, you have my word. Let us let bygones be bygones."

Thornton snorted, grabbing the whiskey bottle. "Your word is not worth a dead rat's whisker. Your days are over, old friend."

The bottle fell from his hand, whiskey spilling out across the table.

Cornelius picked up the bottle, his expression darkening. "Frederick, wake up, you need to stand, walk around. You're drunk."

Frederick mumbled something, trying to focus his eyes on Cornelius. "Train to Manhattan. Call a driver."

"As you wish. Police Chief Merrick is arriving shortly to discuss his upcoming election. As a favor to me, he can drive you to the station. Let us not burn any bridges, old friend. I know it is the whiskey talking, not you. Take a few days to think about it, let me know if you are inclined to accept the new proposition. While you are making your decision, I shall be making a telephone call to Titan, having the oil contract transferred to Grand Union Railway."

Frederick staggered to his feet. "You're right, too much whiskey, never helps. Forget everything I said. I accept your proposition, be richer than Croesus." He grabbed a chair, stumbling against the table.

"Now you're talking sense. Chief Merrick will drive you to the station, you can take the sleeper back to Manhattan, get some rest, sober up. I'll have the butler collect your things, meet us on the porch. Come, I will walk you to the car."

Cornelius took Frederick's arm, walking him outside to the parking area. Simon gave a shout when he saw the police car driving up the gravel road. "It's the ghost car, and Merrick is driving it."

"This is incredible!"

Cornelius helped Frederick down the stairs, opening the passenger door for him, assisting him into the car. "I'll wire you when the oil contract transfer has been finalized. Everything will work out for the best. Not so much whiskey next time."

"Forget what I said, no newspapers. Sorry." Frederick's head was nodding.

Cornelius closed the car door, stepping away. He called out to Police Chief Merrick, "Thanks for your help. When you return we will discuss your upcoming election."

Clara said, "Frederick, can you hear me?"

There was no answer.

"It's dark, I can't see anything."

"I think he passed out from the whiskey, his eyes are

closed."

"I wonder if he was awake when it happened."

"I don't know."

"I can hear the car driving, I just can't see anything."

"It's only fifteen minutes to the station."

Simon heard the brakes squeal, the car lurch to a stop. Frederick's eyes opened. "What? We there?"

"Not yet, sir. I have to put water in the radiator, it's overheating, one of the hoses is leaking."

Frederick's eyes closed again, his head drooping. He gave a start when he heard the car's hood slam shut, mumbling something, his eyes opening a minute later. Simon saw a dark figure standing in the road, twenty feet in front of the car.

Frederick tried to focus on the shadowy figure. "Who is that? Why are they in the road? Out of the way, go. Going to the station."

Simon watched the figure raise one arm, a glint of light reflecting off a shiny object in their hand. There was a brilliant flash of light, then nothing. They were in darkness again.

Simon gave a yelp when he found himself back in the junkyard, gripping Clara's hand, the sound of buzzing insects and rustling leaves drifting across the open field.

The ghost of Frederick Thornton was staring at them from the front seat of the car.

"He shot me dead. I'm a dead man."

Clara nodded. "You've been here a long time, over a hundred years. Your physical body is gone, but your consciousness is still here."

"You are wrong, I have a body, look at the blood. How is this possible?"

"The body you have now is the same body you have in your dreams, your mind created it."

Frederick looked down at his shirt, watching as the blood stains faded away. "The blood is gone."

"You're healing your wounds, waking up."

"If I am truly dead, I fear the price I shall be forced to pay for the things I have done."

Clara said, "You will not have wasted your life if you learned from your mistakes. You are not the same person you were back then. You would make different choices now."

"Perhaps there is truth to what you say, but I have many regrets."

"Everyone has regrets, things they wish they'd done differently."

Frederick stared at his arms, now glowing with a shimmering light.

"What is happening to me? What is this curious glow?"

There was a flash of blazing white light and he was

gone, the old police car empty.

Simon stared at the bullet holes in the seat. "All that and we still don't know who shot him. It was dark, he didn't see who it was."

"It must have been Chief Merrick, he was the only other person there."

"Unless he wasn't. Maybe someone was trying to murder Chief Merrick and they shot Frederick by mistake."

"I guess anything is possible. I'm guessing Chief Merrick had a lot of enemies. We should head back to Caligo Falls."

"Do you really think Cornelius would murder Frederick? It didn't seem like he was still angry at him. He was going to give him the oil contract back."

"Unless he wasn't."

"True."

Simon took out his phone, taking numerous pictures of the old police car, including the license plate and the front seat with the three bullet holes. "We can use these in our brochure."

"What brochure?"

"The one for our paranormal investigation business. We'll need a cool brochure with lots of photos."

"A blood stained car seat with bullet holes in it? Who wants to see something like that?"

"It will show people we're not afraid of murders and ghosts and creepy stuff."

"Let's think about that."

"That's what my mom says when she really means no."

Clara grinned.

"Fine, no bullet holes or blood stained seat, just the old car."

"Deal. When are we going to start this business?"

"We already have, we just don't have any paying clients yet. Or business cards, or a website, or brochures."

"What about college?"

"We can do both, maybe do some ghost work in Boston. There's probably a ton of ghosts floating around those old colleges."

"Let's think about that."

Simon snorted. "I see what you did there."

Clara pointed to something behind Simon. "Simon, look out, here comes the crazy chainsaw killer!"

Simon rolled his eyes. "I was merely speculating on a highly unlikely scenario, based on Billy Whitaker's initial appearance, mainly the red chainsaw he was carrying."

Billy called out, "You folks found the old police car, did you?"

"We did, it's amazing. It would be cool if someone

213

restored it."

"I agree. I'll tow it up by the farmhouse, maybe some-one will buy it."

"It has three bullet holes in the windshield."

"Kids out here shooting stuff. Every stop sign in the county has bullet holes in it."

"Yeah, kids do that."

Clara gave Simon a sideways glance.

"We should go. You have some great old cars here."

"Thanks, stop by again, tell your friends."

Simon and Clara hiked back through the maze of cars toward the farmhouse.

Clara turned to Simon. "Kids do that? They shoot stuff? Really?"

"What? I was just trying to sound like... I don't know... like I wasn't from Brooklyn, like I fit in here."

Clara put her arm around his waist as they walked. "I don't care where you're from. You could be from Mars and I'd still like you."

"How about if I was a giant yellow octopus from Plin-dor?"

"Maybe not so much then. At least now we know what happened between Frederick Thornton and Cor-nelius, why they became bitter enemies."

"The good news is we helped Thornton to move on."

"That is a good thing, better than money."

"Maybe we don't need paying clients. We could be like Edmund and just help the ghosts move on."

"We could do that. Next on the list is Tobias Granger's ghost. We know he was shot in the tunnel, but we don't know who did it or why."

"It had to be Cornelius."

"Why would he shoot the person who saved his life?"

"I don't know, but who else is there?"

"Let's think about this. Tobias was his chauffeur and bodyguard, the man who saved his life. We know his ghost is not in the house and not in the secret tunnel next to his skeleton."

Simon snapped his fingers. "Eureka!"

"This must be big, you're snapping your fingers *and* saying eureka."

"Ask me why."

"Why are you snapping your fingers and saying eureka?"

"Because I just figured out where Tobias is."

"Where?"

"When I was sitting in the old Rolls Royce in the shed I got a chill for about five seconds. I thought it was Frankie, but the Silver Ghost is the car Tobias used to drive."

"And he may have had a strong connection to the car, loved driving it and loved taking care of it. It was his job."

"He's in the old shed, I know he's there, taking care of the car."

"Only one way to find out."

# Chapter 18

Simon and Clara headed back down the highway to Caligo Falls, stopping at several roadside stands to buy veggies for Mrs. Morley.

"I keep thinking about the fourth closet, what Agnes said about a ghost in an unmarked grave near the little cemetery. Do you think it might be Tobias? Maybe he's not the person we think he was, he could be angry at Cornelius for something, maybe for murdering him."

"Agnes said it was a dark spirit, filled with burning rage. That doesn't sound like Tobias. He saved Cornelius' life. I'm sure he's in the old shed."

"Let's go see the ghosts in the fourth closet before we check out the old Rolls Royce. I want to ask them a few more questions. They've been there a long time, they've seen a lot. Maybe they overheard something else about Cornelius and Tobias. Or they know more about Frederick Thornton."

"I should get home. I have to work tomorrow."

"Okay, I'll text you if I find out anything from our old pals in the fourth closet."

"Let me know if Dr. Aldridge is still glowing."

"I will."

Simon dropped Clara off at her house, then headed back to Wilder House, parking the truck in the carriage house. He glanced down the dirt road leading toward the shed, then turned, walking up the hill toward the house. He wanted Clara to be with him when they talked to Tobias, if he was even there. Simon had a curious feeling, as though he was being watched. He slipped on the ghost ring, smiling when he saw Frankie walking next to him.

"Hi Frankie, what are you doing here?"

"Did you go away?"

"I went for a drive with Clara. We were looking for an old car. I won't leave you, I won't go away."

That was the moment Simon realized he would be going away, that he would have to leave Frankie behind when he and Clara went off to college in the fall.

"Say, Frankie, you met the people in the closet down in the basement, right?"

"The smoke hurt my eyes."

"Would you like me to get rid of the smoke for you? You could play with them sometimes. They like kids, I'm sure they would like to be friends with you."

"Will you with me?"

"I'll try to be there, but sometimes Clara and I have things we need to do. I'll tell you what, I'm going to go see them now, do you want to come with me?"

"Yes, please."

"Have you ever seen the old shed that has a big car in it?"

"He was busy."

"There's someone there? Is his name Tobias?"

"I don't know. He was busy."

Simon glanced at his watch, then said, "I have to go have dinner, but after dinner we can go down to the basement and visit the three ghosts."

"What is a ghost?"

Simon's eyes widened. This was unexpected. If Frankie didn't know what a ghost was, then he probably didn't know he had died.

"It's just a different kind of person. They're nice."

"Bye." Frankie vanished, Simon taking off his ring. He opened the front door, stepping into the house, heading to the dining room. His mom, Harrington, and Mrs. Morley were sitting at the dining table.

"Sorry I'm late. It took longer than I thought to get back from Deep River."

"Have a seat before your dinner gets cold."

Kate said, "How did you like Deep River?"

"It was nice, quaint. We went to an old car museum that turned out to be a junkyard, but it was still kind of interesting."

Mrs. Morley gave him a puzzled look. "A car museum in Deep River? Where is it?"

"It's really just an old junkyard on Dead Horse Road."

"I've never heard of Dead Horse Road."

"It's a little dirt road about five miles past Deep River. It's hard to find." Simon was beginning to panic. Why had he mentioned the museum? They'd want to know why they went there, how they found it. His mind was whirling. "We just happened to see it, we took a wrong turn and Clara saw the sign for it so we went in just for fun. They had a bunch of rusty old cars in a big field. They did have a cool old Caligo Falls police car from 1917 though."

Harrington said, "That is an old car. Cornelius Wilder was spending his summers at Wilder House back then. Perhaps a policeman driving that very car gave him a speeding ticket."

Kate laughed. "If only those old cars could talk, the stories they would tell."

"Marvelous stories, I should imagine." Harrington gave Simon a smile.

Simon took a bite of his dinner. "This is really good, Mrs. Morley."

"Thank you, Simon. I made a special dessert for tonight, key lime pie."

"That's the best, thank you so much."

Kate said, "Did you and Clara ever find your secret tunnel in the basement?"

"I forgot to tell you, we did find it. There's a tunnel that goes all the way down to the boathouse. It's safe, it was built with huge wooden support beams. It must have cost a lot. There was nothing in it though, no buried pirate treasure."

Mrs. Morley gave a shiver. "Sounds spooky to me, probably full of ghosts and spiders. Best to keep away from such dark places."

"It was a little spooky."

Harrington said, "But no ghosts?"

Simon shook his head. "Not even one."

The conversation turned to Simon's upcoming college plans, and after some delicious key lime pie he excused himself, saying he was going to look through some of the old stuff in the basement, see if there were any cool antiques hidden away in the closets.

As he was heading for the kitchen door, Harrington called out, "Don't get lost down there."

Kate laughed. "If you do get lost you can just ask a ghost for directions."

Mrs. Morley burst out laughing. "Great heavens, just imagine asking a ghost for directions. It gives me shivers just thinking about it."

Simon headed down to the basement, putting on the

ring. Frankie appeared next to him.

"Hi, Frankie. I'll go into the fourth closet and see if I can get the doctor to stop smoking his pipe."

"It hurts my nose."

Simon picked up his flashlight, stepping into the closet, pulling on the rope to open the door, calling out, "Hello, it's me, Simon."

He stepped into the room, spotting Agnes Holloway and Professor Barnsworth, but not Dr. Aldridge. Simon was getting a bad feeling.

Agnes' face was pale, even for a ghost. "Hello, Simon. How nice of you to stop by for a visit."

"Where's Dr. Aldridge?"

Agnes' shoulders sank, her body shaking. She turned away, covering her face with her hands.

Professor Barnsworth's face was grim. "He's gone, there was nothing we could do. He tried to fight it, but it was too much for him, he grew brighter and brighter, and then he was gone."

Agnes wiped her eyes. "There are only two of us now. How can a League of Spectral Tourists have only two members? What will we do?"

Simon said, "I'm so sorry. He was really nice, such a good sense of humor."

"Yes, he would so often make us laugh with the most humorous anecdotes about his time as a surgeon. I don't know how we shall go on without him."

Simon was wondering what could possibly be funny about being a surgeon in the 1860s.

The professor turned to look at something behind Simon. "Good heavens, we have another visitor."

Simon spun around, his fear vanishing when he saw Frankie standing behind him.

"This is Frankie Doyle. He was in the 1918 pandemic. So was his mom, Rose Doyle."

"Yes, we are aware of this." The professor gave Frankie a friendly smile. "Hello, young man. It's very nice to finally meet you. You've popped in here before, but only for a brief moment."

"He said the pipe smoke hurt his nose."

"It was quite pungent, wasn't it?"

Agnes daubed her eyes with a white handkerchief. "I shall miss it dearly."

"As shall I."

A novel idea popped into Simon's head. "Just a thought, what would you think about Frankie joining your League of Spectral Tourists? He doesn't really have any other friends except me and Clara."

Professor Barnsworth glanced over at Agnes. "That would be wonderful under other circumstances, but sadly, we shall have to decline. The timing of your request is most unfortuitous."

"Because of Dr. Aldridge?"

The professor shook his head. "There is more bad news, I'm afraid."

"What kind of bad news?"

Agnes pulled off one of her white gloves, holding up one hand.

"Your hand is glowing."

"I fear my time here is limited."

The professor pulled up one of his sleeves, his arm surrounded by a white shimmering glow. "You are bearing witness to the final days of the League of Spectral Tourists, I'm afraid. We have one or two weeks at the most, if that."

Simon wasn't sure how to respond. This was something he had never really thought about, ghosts moving on, leaving their ghost friends behind. It was really just another form of dying, just as sad to those left behind. He said, "I'm sorry. I know this probably doesn't help at all, but the place you go to when you move on is supposed to be really amazing."

"You are correct, young man, it is beauty beyond comprehension, exquisite in every conceivable way. And yet, we chose to stay here in the comfort of what we know, enjoying the company of old friends. Sentimental foolishness, I suppose."

"It's not foolish at all. I think what you've

accomplished here is amazing. The paintings that Edmund did of other worlds could change everything."

"I fear they will be viewed only as fantastical art, nothing more. The time for this world to acknowledge the existence of other living worlds is yet to come."

"One day people will realize what a treasure they are, but for now, I know what they are, and Clara knows what they are. That's something."

"Perhaps you shall be a beacon of light in this world. One never really knows about such things."

"That's why I'm majoring in physics, I want to understand the deeper nature of this world."

"And so you shall, my young friend. Of this I am certain."

Agnes gave a wistful smile. "Perhaps you and Clara would stop by for another visit before we leave?"

"Of course. She's working today, but we can stop by tomorrow."

"Wonderful. I know you will have a marvelous life together, both of you."

"She's my best friend."

"I can see that." Agnes stepped over to Frankie, bending down, giving him a hug. "It was lovely to meet you, Frankie. I wish we could spend more time with you, but Professor Barnsworth and I shall be going away for a very long time, traveling to another world."

"My mama went away."

"I know she did, and it's very sad when that happens. You must miss her dreadfully, with all your heart. One day you will see her again, that is something I know to be true. Take comfort in that, dear one."

Simon said, "I should probably go. I'll call Clara and tell her everything. We'll come visit tomorrow."

"That would be marvelous."

"I just had a quick question. We think there's a ghost down at the shed where the old Rolls Royce is parked. Do you know who it is?"

"We do, and it is time you heard his story. It is a vital piece of the puzzle you have been searching for, answers you must find on your own."

"He's not scary, like the one at the cemetery?"

"He is confused and hurt, but not scary, not angry."

"That's good to know, thanks. We'll see you tomorrow."

Simon headed back upstairs, Frankie trailing behind him. He glanced back at Frankie, giving him a reassuring smile, but with the impending departure of Agnes and Professor Barnsworth, he had no idea what Frankie was going to do when he and Clara went off to college.

# Chapter 19

Simon ran up the grand staircase to his room, texting Clara.

*Dr. Aldridge is gone, moved on. It was awful, Agnes was crying. Both of them are beginning to glow. They want us to visit them tomorrow, said they only have a week or two left.*

*That's so sad, they were all such good friends. I'll come by in the morning, no work tomorrow.*

*They said there's a ghost in the old shed, but wouldn't say who it was. Not scary though, just sad and hurt.*

*People never think about ghosts being sad, having feelings.*

*I know, it felt like Dr. Aldridge had died. I thought maybe Frankie could stay with them, but they said they won't be here much longer.*

*Too bad, it was a good idea. Gotta go, customers.*

*See you tomorrow morning.*

*See you.*

Simon was sitting at the kitchen table the next morning when he heard the doorbell ring. "That's Clara. I'll get it."

"We have plenty of food if she hasn't had breakfast."

"Thanks, I'll tell her."

Simon ran to the front door, pulling it open, stopping short when he saw the police uniform. It was Sergeant Rogers from the Caligo Falls Police Department.

Simon stammered, "Oh, hi, sorry, um, I was expecting someone else. Sergeant Rogers, right?"

"Right. I had a few questions for you about that plate number you were trying to find."

"Oh, right, I sort of forgot about that."

"You remembered my name but not why you came to see me?"

"No, sorry, um, I was confused. What about the plate?"

"I got interested in it. Not a lot of crime around here. I did some digging through the old records. The car was purchased by Police Chief Merrick in 1917, his personal patrol car. It was also part of a murder investigation, a man was shot in the car, three shots fired through the windshield. The car was kept as evidence until it was sold. Chief Merrick testified that he saw the perpetrator, a man named Josiah Finch, but Mr. Finch took his own life before they could arrest him."

Simon nodded. "I read an old newspaper article about that. Josiah Finch was Bobby Finch's grandfather."

"He works at the general store?"

"Yes, super nice guy. He said his grandfather was an alcoholic."

"You have been doing your homework. Did you ever locate the car?"

"Actually we did find it, kind of a funny story." Simon was beginning to panic.

"How did you find it?"

"Well, you said it was sold to C.Whitaker and D.River in 1924. We figured out that D.River wasn't a person, it was a place, Deep River, north of here. We went online and found an antique car museum in Deep River owned by Billy Whitaker, the grandson of Carl Whitaker, the man who bought the car. The car is still there in a field, untouched, three bullet holes in the windshield. It was covered by an old tarp."

"No kidding? That's good detective work, I'm impressed."

"Thanks, Clara and I spent a lot of time searching for it."

"What do you know about Chief Merrick?"

"What do you mean?"

"About what happened to him?"

"I found an article saying that he had retired in 1924 and moved to California, that Cornelius Wilder bought him a little house on the coast to thank him for his distinguished service to Caligo Falls."

"What do you think about that?"

"To be honest, it sounds a little off."

"Why?"

"From everything we've heard about him, Cornelius Wilder was not a nice guy, he wouldn't buy someone a house just to be nice. We thought the house was probably a payment for something, or just a way to get him out of Caligo Falls."

"I could say the same thing about Chief Merrick, not a nice a guy. Apparently he sent quite a few people to prison who shouldn't have gone. Things were different back then. He was also the sole witness to the murder, sending up a whole pile of red flags for me."

Simon decided it was probably best not to mention that he and Clara were also witnesses to the murder. "Are you saying it's possible that Josiah Finch didn't murder Frederick Thornton?"

Sergeant Roger's eyes narrowed imperceptibly. "You should probably tell me how you know Frederick

Thornton's name."

"Oh, right, Edmund Wilder kept a whole bunch of newspaper clippings from back then, one of them with a photograph of Thornton, saying he was Cornelius Wilder's partner. We also found an article online in the Caligo Falls Gazette archives about Frederick Thornton being Cornelius Wilder's business partner for about ten years, until they split up. And there was an article about Thornton's murder, how Walter Merrick had been the only witness."

"Interesting. Where is this old car museum located?"

"It's on Dead Horse Road, about five miles north of Deep River. It's kind of hard to find, it's just a narrow dirt road. Billy Whitaker calls it a museum, but it's really a junkyard."

Sergeant Rogers laughed. "There's a lot of that up here. You ever going to tell me how you knew the plate number?"

"Um, you probably don't want to know."

"Not if it has something to do with Wilder House or ghosts."

"You probably don't want to know."

"Let me know if you find anything else interesting. I'm going to keep digging. I'm getting a feeling about this, and it's not a good one." He turned when he heard the car coming up the driveway. "Looks like your friend

Clara Barley is here. Have a great day, stay out of trouble."

"We will, thanks."

Clara was sitting in the car, her eyes on Sergeant Rogers. He smiled at her, tipping his hat. "Have a great day."

"Thanks."

Clara jumped out of the car, joining Simon on the porch.

"What was he doing here? What did he want?"

"He's been doing some research on the ghost car. It's sounding like he doesn't think Josiah Finch was guilty. I guess Chief Merrick had a reputation for putting innocent people in prison."

"What did you tell him?"

"Nothing he couldn't find in old newspaper articles."

"Good. Let's go see Agnes and Professor Barnsworth."

Simon turned toward the front door, spotting Mrs. Morley peering out the window. This was not good, she'd seen Sergeant Rogers talking to him.

The front door opened, Kate and Mrs. Morley stepping out.

"Simon, why were you talking to a policeman?"

"He had a question about the old Caligo Falls police car at the junkyard. He was interested in it."

"How did he know to ask you about it?"

Simon was prepared for the question. "The original plate was still on the car, so we asked him about it. He said the police department bought the car in 1917."

"I was afraid you were in some kind of trouble."

"Not a chance, they got no proof I robbed that bank."

Mrs. Morley gave a loud squawk. "Robbing a bank, good heavens, what a thought! I don't know how your mother puts up with you."

Kate laughed. "I don't know either, Mrs. Morley."

Simon and Clara headed down to the basement, grabbing a flashlight, weaving their way through the furniture to the fourth door. Simon slipped on his ring while Clara pulled on the rope, the door sliding open.

Simon's heart sank when he saw the dark shadowy empty room. Clara put one hand over her mouth, her eyes wide.

"They're gone. They're both gone."

"I didn't get to say goodbye to them."

Simon took his ring off, then put it back on, hoping they would still be there. They weren't.

Frankie appeared in front of them, looking up at Clara. "They went away. They said goodbye."

Simon stepped over to the rack of paintings, pulling one out, studying it. "I can't believe they're gone. I was just talking to them."

Clara said, "I know."

"What should we do with these paintings?"

"Look on the back, see if Edmund made any notes about them."

Simon flipped it over. "There's a card stapled to the frame."

*The apocalyptic world of Varmoran,*
*as seen by Professor Barnsworth in 1972.*

"It doesn't give a location, say how far it is from Earth."

"I don't think they knew, they traveled there instantly."

"Let's move all the paintings upstairs to his studio."

"What will you do with them?"

"I don't know, maybe we should make an announcement that we discovered a group of lost paintings by Edmund Wilder. They're different from anything else he's done."

"People will just think it's fantasy sci-fi art."

"It doesn't matter, people will see them. It's not something that should be hidden away."

"Maybe Marion Jaggers could help. She knows a lot of people in New York."

After they had carried all the paintings up to the studio, Simon closed the door to the fourth closet with a long sigh. He called his mom down to Edmund's studio to look at the paintings.

"They're beautiful. You're certain Edmund painted these?"

"I am. They were stored in one of the closets."

"They're lovely, even if they are imaginary places. That's a good idea about having an art exhibition, putting them on display for the public to see. I'll call Marion and ask her about it. Maybe she can arrange a show in New York. People will be very interested in these."

"That's what we were thinking; Marion knows a lot of people there."

Kate picked up one of the paintings, flipping it over. "He even made up names for the worlds he painted. This one is Plindor, as seen by Agnes Victoria Holloway in 1968. That name sounds familiar, I think I've heard it before."

Kate pulled out her phone, tapping on it. "Here it is, she was a well known writer in the 1930s. She died in 1952 though, so she wasn't alive in 1968. It's odd that Edmund would use her name. Maybe he knew her, and the painting was his way of remembering her. He probably knew a lot of writers and artists."

"Probably." Simon glanced over at Clara.

Kate said, "I'm going to go call Marion, see what she thinks about it."

"We're going to check out that cool old car down in the shed. It's a 1917 Rolls Royce Silver Ghost."

"Sounds valuable. We should donate those cars to a museum sometime."

Simon and Clara headed outside, walking down the hill toward the carriage house.

"Are you ready for this?"

Simon shrugged. "I guess so. Agnes said it wasn't a scary ghost."

"It has to be Tobias Granger, who else could it be?"

They strolled down the narrow dirt road to the moss covered shed, Simon eyeing the chipped and peeling paint.

"I'm going to have someone repair the shed, fix it all up, paint it."

"Or you could park your truck up at the house and move the Rolls Royce into the carriage house."

"Words I never thought I would hear in my lifetime."

"Words I never thought I would say in my lifetime."

Simon approached the shed door, gripping the handle, pulling it open, the hinges squealing loudly.

He pulled the tarp off the car, Clara eyeing the magnificent vehicle. "It really is beautiful, they don't make cars like this anymore."

"They all look the same now, it's kind of sad." Simon took the ghost ring out of his pocket, Clara taking his hand.

"Do it."

Simon slipped the ring on, the two friends stepping back when they saw the enormous man polishing one of the fenders with a white cloth, the man seemingly unaware of their presence.

"It's Tobias. Same chauffeur's uniform, same leather boots, and the same guy I saw in the newspaper photo. He's huge, he must be six-foot-six."

"Just like the skeleton."

"Right."

Simon called out, "Tobias? Tobias Granger?"

There was no response. Clara said, "He's a sleeper."

Simon and Clara stepped across the straw covered floor, approaching Tobias, studying his clothing. Simon stopped when he saw the back of his black chauffeur's uniform.

"Clara, look at this."

She studied Tobias' uniform. "Two holes in the back of his coat. I'm guessing they're bullet holes?"

"It's hard to see it against the black coat, but there are blood stains. Someone shot him in the back."

"The poor man. Why would someone do that?"

"Let's see if we can find out."

Simon reached out, touching the chauffeur's arm.

The shed vanished, Simon finding himself in a

cluttered office, stacks of papers lying on a battered old metal desk, racks of well used tools hanging on the walls. There was a calendar next to them, a lovely young lady on display, the year was 1916.

Simon was shaking the hand of a burly man chewing on a cigar, his black hair slicked back.

"You keep them working, no slackers, no fighting, no drinking on the job. You gotta keep them in line, no excuses, you ain't their friend no more, you're their boss, the foreman. You got it? No favors to no one. You got no friends here."

"Got it."

"Screw it up and you're gone."

"I got it."

He handed Tobias a brass badge. "Here's your foreman's badge. Wear it all the time, don't take it off. Shows them who you are. Don't let them forget. You do whatever you got to do to get the line built, we look the other way."

Simon watched Tobias reach out and take the badge, pinning it onto his stained canvas jacket. "What's my pay?"

"Extra five dollars a week."

"Nice. I can use it to buy that mansion I wanted."

The man behind the desk snorted loudly. "Get out of here, back to work. The big boss gets here this afternoon, inauguration for the new line, then it's back to the grindstone."

Tobias turned, stepping outside into a bustling construction site, men laying tracks, the clanging sound of heavy sledge hammers pounding railroad spikes, a dozen old fashioned trucks filled with railroad ties being unloaded by grizzled, hard looking men. Two flatbed train cars carrying sections of steel track were being offloaded with a tall crane.

Tobias spoke to them for the first time. "This was the day I made foreman. It was a good day, I worked hard for it, never slacked off, no drinking."

"I'm Clara Barley and this is my friend Simon. We're reliving your memory. Do you understand that?"

"I was remembering the days before I met Cornelius Wilder. It was another life, simpler, not like it is now."

The construction site seemed to ripple, everything turning black for a moment.

Simon heard the cigar-chewing man bellow out, "All the foremen up front! Keep an eye out for trouble. Anything happens to Wilder and you're dead men."

Tobias stepped through the crowd, taking his place near the colorfully festooned podium, reading the hand lettered sign standing beside it.

## Midland & Southern Railways
## Grand Inauguration of the new
## St. Louis to Chicago Line
## July 18, 1916

A uniformed brass band struck up a lively tune, their polished instruments sparkling in the afternoon sun as a group of dignitaries sporting beaver top hats emerged from the newly constructed train depot, walking over to the podium.

Tobias moved closer to the podium, hoping to get a better look at the owner of the line, Cornelius Wilder. He wondered what it would be like to be that rich, be able to buy anything he wanted.

Cornelius stepped up to the podium, raising both arms, his voice booming out. "We would be nothing without the likes of workers like you! You built all this!"

The crowd cheered wildly, a few tossing their woolen caps in the air. Cornelius stepped around the podium, moving closer to the throng of workers, now only a few feet away from Tobias.

Cornelius looked up at Tobias, calling out, "Look at the size of this giant of a man! I tell you, folks, I wouldn't want to face this fellow in a boxing ring! I'll wager he keeps all you slackers in line!"

The workers roared with laughter. Simon was impressed with Cornelius' ability to manipulate the rowdy crowd.

Tobias turned, spotting a ragged man pushing his way through the crowd toward the podium. He was only fifteen feet away when he pulled out a black revolver, aiming it at Cornelius, shrieking, "You took my land! Die like a dog!"

Tobias felt someone grab the back of his coat, pulling him to one side. It was Cornelius, pulling Tobias in front of him, using him as a shield.

The man with the gun stumbled, there was a bright flash, a cloud of black smoke, the lead bullet hitting Tobias in the leg, shattering his femur, the pain excruciating. He tumbled over, falling to the ground. It would take months for his leg to fully heal, months more until he could walk normally again.

The crowd went mad, grabbing the pistol from the assailant, pushing him to the ground, pummeling him, kicking him, cursing him. Uniformed police ran over to him, dragging the unconscious man away by his arms.

Cornelius hollered, "This brave man needs a doctor! He saved my life, jumped in front of me! There's a real hero, folks!"

The crowd cheered for Tobias, unaware that Cornelius had used him as a human shield.

# Chapter 20

Simon was lying in a hospital bed, his leg in a full length plaster cast, throbbing with a pain that would not go away.

Clara said, "This hurts. Don't ever shoot me in the leg."

"I'll try not to. You saw what happened? What Cornelius did?"

"I saw. The newspaper article said Tobias was a hero, that he'd jumped in front of Cornelius to save his life. Not true. Cornelius grabbed Tobias and hid behind him. If the shooter hadn't tripped, Tobias could have been killed."

Simon turned when he heard a door open, two nurses in starched white uniforms and nursing caps stepping into the room, Cornelius striding in behind them.

"There he is, the man of the hour, the hero they're all talking about. It's in the Tribune, front page news, son. You're a first class bona fide hero."

Tobias nodded, knowing full well he was not a hero.

Cornelius said, "Listen, son, I'm the kind of man who

rewards good deeds. I could use a big fellow like you. How would you like to be my bodyguard? You'll have to learn how to drive a car, you'd be my chauffeur. You'll earn ten times what you earn now, live in a mansion, all the food you want, wear a sharp uniform, high class. What do you think, hero?"

Tobias managed a grin, despite his aching leg. "When do I start?"

"That's the way, well done. Soon as your leg heals I'll have someone teach you how to drive. Got a brand spanking new Rolls Royce Silver Ghost, cost more than three houses."

The hospital room vanished, replaced by the interior of a luxurious 1917 Rolls Royce Silver Ghost, Simon at the steering wheel.

"Hey, I'm driving the Silver Ghost. How cool is this?"

"Don't you mean Tobias is driving it?"

"I'm watching him, learning how to drive it. I should drive the Rolls around Caligo Falls."

"That would really impress people, you'd make a lot of new friends."

"Probably not the kind I want though."

Tobias pulled the Rolls Royce into the gravel parking area at Wilder House, his eyes on the gleaming police car, the front seat currently occupied by Chief Walter Merrick.

243

Tobias said, "I remember this day. Nothing good ever came of a visit from Chief Merrick."

Simon said, "Were Chief Merrick and Cornelius good friends?"

"Mr. Wilder has many associates across the country who are more than willing to do his bidding, always for a price. Chief Merrick is one of those men, Mr. Wilder's lackey in Caligo Falls. All it took was a sizable donation to Chief Merrick's election campaign, and now he does whatever Mr. Wilder asks of him."

"Do you know anything about the death of Mr. Wilder's partner, Frederick Thornton?"

"Only what I read in the newspapers, that he was shot in cold blood by a local man who was intoxicated at the time. The man took his own life before he could be arrested."

Tobias opened the passenger door, Cornelius emerging from the Rolls Royce, waving to Chief Merrick, motioning for him to follow him into the house. The two men strode up the stairs onto the covered porch, making their way to the front door.

Tobias drove the car down to the carriage house, spending the next half hour polishing the Silver Ghost until it shined.

He walked back up the hill, entering Wilder House through the servants' entrance, stepping through the pantry into the kitchen, taking a seat at the table.

An older woman wearing a white apron smiled at him. "Ready for dinner?"

"Famished, it's been a long day."

"Is there any other kind?"

Tobias laughed. He was eating dinner when the butler stepped in, slumping down in a chair. "I fear it is going to be a late night."

"They're drinking again?"

The butler nodded. "Heavily. Chief Merrick is a dreadful influence on Mr. Wilder."

"He's a dark one, he is."

"I would not choose to get on the wrong side of such a man as him."

"Would you happen to know what time Mr. Wilder will be needing the car in the morning?"

"I am uncertain, especially if they continue drinking as they are."

"Perhaps I should knock on the door and ask him?"

"You are wearing your uniform, so it is permitted, but be quick about it. They're in the sitting room. Say nothing untoward regarding Chief Merrick, be on your best behavior no matter what he says."

"Of course."

Tobias rose up, putting his dishes in the sink, then headed through the kitchen door into the front hall, making his way to the sitting room, the heavy oaken door closed. He could hear the two men laughing, more than likely at one of Merrick's seemingly endless collection of vulgar anecdotes. Tobias curled his lip. There was something supremely unlikable about Chief Merrick, his stories filled with a dark and cruel humor, always revolving around the suffering of others.

He rapped gently on the door, but Merrick's voice had grown louder than ever, his words slurred, hard to understand, muffled by the solid oak door. Tobias stood patiently at the door, hands clasped behind his back, waiting for the voices to die down. They stopped abruptly. Tobias was raising his hand to knock on the door when it swung open, a drunken Walter Merrick standing unsteadily in the doorway, his face blotchy and red, Tobias attempting to conceal his revulsion for the man.

"What is it? Why you standing there?"

"I did not wish to interrupt you, sir, but I was wondering what time Mr. Wilder might be needing the car tomorrow?"

Cornelius called out, "Noon will be fine, Tobias."

"Thank you, sir."

Merrick gave Tobias a darkly suspicious look, his voice low. "You been listening? Snooping?"

"No, sir, it is not my place to do so."

Merrick scowled, then shut the door, Tobias standing

silently, listening to the men's inaudible whispers before heading down the hallway to the back stairs and up to his room.

Simon said, "Merrick is terrifying."

Clara said, "Did you see his eyes? So frightening."

Tobias pulled off his leather boots, then carefully hung up his chauffeur's uniform in the wardrobe, climbing into bed.

Simon and Clara were surrounded by darkness as Tobias slept. Simon whispered, "He didn't know about Chief Merrick framing Josiah Finch, or who really shot Frederick Thornton."

Simon abruptly found himself standing next to the Rolls Royce in the parking area, Mr. Wilder walking down the front steps.

Cornelius approached Tobias, speaking in low, conspiratorial tones. "I'm going to require your services for a short time, moving some crates down in the tunnel, just arrived yesterday. This is not something anyone else in the house should know about."

"Of course, sir, I completely understand."

"Good. Follow me."

They headed into the house, Cornelius leading the way down the marble staircase to the front hall of the basement, then on to the storage area, entering into the tunnel through the second closet. Cornelius pulled the X-shaped key from his pocket, opening the steel door.

"The cases of whiskey are at the end of the tunnel near the boathouse. Bring them all up and stack them on the shelves. Be careful, they came all the way from Scotland. Cost me a fortune to get them here, most of it bribes."

"I shall handle them with kid gloves, sir."

"I'll be in the sitting room, knock on the door, let me know when you're done."

"Of course, sir."

Cornelius left the room, Tobias making his way down the tunnel, eyeing the crates of whiskey stacked beneath the trap door that led to the boat house.

Simon said, "That is a lot of whiskey."

Clara added, "It's also illegal. They outlawed alcohol in 1920."

Tobias picked up one of the crates, carrying it carefully through the tunnel to the secret room, setting it gingerly on one of the iron shelves.

Clara said, "Tobias, do you like Mr. Wilder?"

"He is driven by avarice and a lust for power, but he has treated me better than most."

"Is it because of what happened when the assailant tried to shoot him?"

"This job was his way of assuring that I said nothing to the newspapers about his actions. For my part, I happily accepted our unspoken agreement of silence, the new position paying far more than my former position as foreman, with far more benefits."

It took almost an hour to move all the crates, Tobias finally setting the last one on the heavy iron shelves. He stood for moment, his eyes on the twenty-four crates of whiskey.

"Why would one person need so much whiskey?"

There was a sudden flash of light in the room, a deafening roar, Simon feeling like someone had slammed him in the back with an iron bar. He looked down at the blood seeping out of his shirt.

Tobias touched the blood. "Why am I bleeding?"

There was a second flash of light, then darkness.

Simon and Clara were back in the shed, standing next to the Rolls Royce Silver Ghost, Tobias still polishing the car with a soft white cloth.

"Tobias, do you remember what happened to you after you heard the loud noises in the tunnel?"

"Nothing happened. The pain vanished as if by magic, and I never was able to discover the cause of it. I went about my business, taking care of Mr. Wilder's car. Mr. Wilder likes the car to shine like a jewel."

Clara said, "Did you ever tell Cornelius you had finished moving all the crates?"

Tobias set the white cloth down on the car's fender. "That is odd, I have no recollection of talking to him about that. I should run and tell him. I don't know how I could forget such a thing."

"Do you know what year this is?"

Tobias gave him a curious look. "How could you not know the year? It is 1924."

Clara stepped closer to Tobias. "Tobias, this is going to be hard for you to understand, but you died that day in the tunnel. The flashes of light and the loud noises were gunshots. Someone shot you twice in the back, one of the bullets passing through you. Do you remember the blood on your chest?"

Tobias glanced down at his uniform, a blood stain appearing on his jacket and shirt. "There is blood, but I am not dead, I'm right here, talking to you." He touched his hand to his bloodstained shirt.

Simon picked up a wooden board from the floor, passing it through Tobias, a look of horror crossing Tobias' face. "What is this? I am a ghostly apparition?"

"You are still Tobias Granger, but you left your physical body behind over a hundred years ago."

"Impossible, it has been no more than a day or two since I moved the crates."

"You have been in this shed for over a hundred years. Go up to Wilder House, look around, visit the Caligo Falls town center, look at all the modern cars. Look up in the sky at the huge airplanes passing overhead."

Tobias stared at Simon. "If this is truly so, what shall become of me?"

"I have a friend named Robert Sawyer who can help you. He died a few years ago. He can tell you everything you need to know. You can do anything you want now, you can fly to Paris, walk through walls, go visit the moon if you want."

Tobias pushed his hand tentatively through the shed wall. He jumped back in surprise, looking at Simon. "My hand went through the wall."

Clara said, "Try walking through the wall."

Tobias stepped forward, passing through the wall, Simon and Clara running outside.

There was of look of disbelief on Tobias' face. "I am a ghostly specter."

Clara pointed to Tobias' hand. "Simon, his hand is glowing."

Tobias held up his hand, studying the curious glow. "What ever would cause my hand to–"

There was a flash of light and Tobias was gone.

"We woke him up, he remembered."

"He didn't see who shot him. It could have been anyone."

"Maybe Robert Sawyer can help us. He helped us locate Darlene's old boyfriend."

"I wish the League of Spectral Tourists was still here."

"Do you think Frankie would know anything?"

Simon shook his head. "I doubt it, he spent most of his time in the basement playing with his wooden horse, waiting for his mom to come back."

"There is one other person we could talk to."

"For the record, we're not going to the unmarked grave behind the little cemetery. Not going to happen. You heard what the professor said, the ghost there is a dark hearted being filled with vile thoughts of revenge. It's trapped inside itself. I don't even want to look at it."

"Fine, we'll go talk to Robert. He might know something about the ghost in the cemetery."

"You are referring to the ghost we are never going to talk to? Ever? That one?"

Clara grinned. "That's the one."

# Chapter 21

The next morning found Simon was sitting on the porch, basking in the warmth of the summer sun, his thoughts turning to the ghost behind the old cemetery. They agreed they would never talk to it, but who was it? Why couldn't he let this go? The murders took place a hundred years ago, nobody cared about them anymore, it was ancient history. He should just forget about it, enjoy the rest of the summer with Clara. Go swimming, go to the movies, go on hikes. Maybe the ghost in the cemetery was Cornelius. It sounded a little like him, angry, wanting revenge. He might still be angry about Frederick's plan to blackmail him, threatening to reveal his underhanded business dealings to the newspapers. There was also the unlikely possibility that it was Walter Merrick. The problem was, he had moved to California in 1924, so it didn't make a lot of sense that he would have come back to haunt the little cemetery.

Simon groaned. "Let it go. It doesn't matter. Do something fun."

Simon decided to go up to the widow's watch on the

roof and just enjoy the view, relax, think about how lucky he was, about all the wonderful things that had happened over the last four months, how lucky he was to have met Clara.

He headed up to the third floor, climbing up the stairs to the metal door that opened to the widow's watch, squinting in the bright sunlight as he stepped outside.

"This view is amazing. The lake looks nice and calm. I should see if Clara wants to go swimming. We can dive off the boat, have some fun, not think about crazy murders. Darlene is gone, so no ghosts at the lake. I should make sure I didn't miss any."

He pulled the ghost ring from his pocket, slipping it on, gazing down at the lake, spinning around when he saw something move in the corner of his eye. It was Frankie.

"Hi, Frankie. How are you today? Are you enjoying this beautiful relaxing carefree summer day?"

"Mama was on a big boat in the ocean."

"Really? That must have been fun."

"The waves were big. It was scary."

"Big waves would be scary."

"Do you have a boat?"

Simon suspected where Frankie was going with this. "I have a little rowboat down at the lake. Would you like to go for a ride in it?"

"I can ride in it?"

"Of course you can. How about this, I'll go put on some shorts, then meet you down at the boathouse, take you for a ride in the boat. How does that sound? Fun and relaxing, right?"

Frankie vanished.

Simon laughed. "I'll take that as a yes."

An hour later Simon was sliding the heavy boathouse doors open, Frankie standing next to him. He set the oars in the old wooden rowboat, then pushed it down the ramp into the water, hopping into it, pushing off. Frankie appeared on the bow of the boat, a huge grin on his face.

Simon smiled. He never imagined a six-year-old ghost would be so excited about riding in an old wooden rowboat on a little lake in Caligo Falls. Simple pleasures were the best. One thing he knew for certain, there was a long list of simple pleasures, but the list did not include talking to terrifying ghosts who lived behind creepy cemeteries.

Frankie pointed to the oars. "What are those?"

"They're called oars, I use them to make the boat go."

Simon rowed out into the lake, showing Frankie how the oars worked. He was enjoying the warmth of the sun, wondering if Frankie could feel it.

"Isn't the bright sun nice and warm today?"

Frankie leaned over the boat, peering into the water.

"What is in the water?"

"Fish live down there. They just swim around and do fish stuff."

"I think I see a fish doing fish stuff."

Simon laughed. "You were lucky to see one."

That brief conversation was the catalyst for Simon's two unexpected revelations. The first revelation was that he would be a good dad, that it would be fun teaching a kid about things like fish swimming in a lake doing fish stuff. The second revelation was something else entirely. Eureka times infinity, plus one.

He pulled his phone out, texting Clara.

*I just had the best idea in the history of best ideas in the known universe. Can I pick you up at lunchtime?*

*Have you been drinking whiskey?*

*What?*

*You decided we should talk to the cemetery ghost?*

*Not even close. This is WAY better.*

*What is it?*

*It's a surprise, that's what.*

*See you at noon. My favorite color is green and I wear size 7 Jordans.*

*Nice try. See you soon. Just to reiterate, best idea ever.*

Simon slipped his phone back into his pocket.

"Say, Frankie, have you ever ridden in a car?"

Frankie shook his head. "Is it scary?"

"Not at all, it's really fun. You sit in the car, look out the window and watch everything go by. Maybe we'll see a moose or a deer or even a big raven. Ravens are really smart birds."

"Do you have a car and a boat?"

"I have an old truck that I like to drive. I thought we could take a nice drive with Clara today. You like Clara, don't you?"

Frankie nodded. "I like Clara."

"Let's row around the lake for a while, then go for a ride in the truck with Clara. How does that sound?"

"Will a fish jump into the boat?"

"No, they don't do that, they just swim around in the water and do fish stuff."

"I don't want a fish to bite me."

"They don't do that, there's nothing to worry about, I promise."

An hour later they were rolling down the highway

toward the town center, Frankie gazing out the window.

"I see a car."

"It's a nice new one. Shiny. It looks expensive."

"Where is the moose?"

"I don't see any right now. Sometimes you see them, but not very often. You have to be lucky to see one, just like when you saw the fish."

"Is that your house? I see another car."

"No, I just have one house, the one we live in. That house belongs to someone else."

"Who?"

"I don't know. Someone nice though, they have a pretty garden, lots of nice flowers."

Simon pulled the truck into the grocery store parking lot, Clara standing near the front door, waving to him.

"There's Clara. Move closer to me so she has room to sit. I'm going to surprise her."

Clara climbed into the truck, closing the door. "Okay, what's this incredible idea?"

"I think we should hold hands before I tell you."

Clara laughed, reaching over to take his hand, giving a shriek when she saw Frankie sitting between them.

Frankie vanished, reappearing in the back seat, his eyes wide.

Clara said, "I'm sorry, Frankie, I didn't mean to scare you. I was so surprised to see you that I shrieked. I always shriek when I see someone I really like."

Frankie reappeared on the front seat. "I rode in a boat."

"Wow, really? You rode in a boat?"

Simon nodded. "I took him for a ride in the rowboat. It was fun. I think he saw a fish."

"It didn't bite me."

"That's good."

Simon said, "I told him fish don't bite people, they just swim around in the water and do fish stuff."

"Your greatest idea in the world was to give Frankie a boat ride and a ride in your truck? That was nice of you."

"Better than that, I was thinking that you and I and Frankie could go visit our old friend Robert Sawyer. Wouldn't that be nice?"

Clara stared at him for a moment, then raised both eyebrows. "That *is* a very good idea, Simon. A very, very good idea. I bet Robert will really like Frankie. He doesn't have any friends except for Dorothy."

"Exactly."

Simon started the truck, heading north on the highway, slowing down when they reached Robert's old house, pulling over to the side of the road, shutting off the engine. Simon called out, "Hey, Robert Sawyer, we need to talk to you, it's important."

Robert appeared three seconds later in front of the truck, sporting green and yellow checkered shorts, a blue sleeveless shirt, and a straw hat.

Simon and Clara climbed out of the truck, Frankie hiding behind Simon, peering out at Robert.

"What's so important? I was on the beach in the south of France. You should see Dorothy's bathing suit. Yowza."

"Sounds like fun."

Robert spotted Frankie, his eyes narrowing. "Who's that?"

"Oh, this is our friend Frankie. He's super nice. He was in the 1918 Spanish Flu pandemic. So was his mom. He's been living in Wilder House since then, hoping his mom will come back for him."

Robert studied Simon and Clara for a moment, then said, "I know exactly what you're doing, and it's not going to work."

Frankie looked up at Robert. "I rode in a boat and saw a fish."

Robert eyed Frankie. "You saw a fish? What kind of fish?"

"A little one. It didn't bite me. Is that your house? Do you have a car?"

"That's a lot of questions. I don't have a car, I ride my bike. That used to be my house, but now it's not. I live

260

somewhere else now that I'm–" He stopped, turning to Simon. "Does he know about, you know, his current status?"

Simon shook his head. "No, he's just waiting for his mom. We're his only friends."

Robert frowned, kneeling down in front of Frankie. "How old are you, kid?"

"Six."

"What's with the wooden horse? Who gave it to you?"

"Mama."

"It's nice. Do you have any other toys? A bicycle? Basketball? Toy cars?"

Frankie shook his head, holding the toy horse close to him. "I have a horse."

A ghostly basketball appeared in front of Robert. He bounced it up and down on the pavement. "It's called a basketball." He handed it to Frankie.

Frankie took the ball, then dropped it, watching it bounce and roll away, a grin crossing his face. He ran and picked it up, bouncing it again, then brought it back to Robert, holding it out for him to take.

"You keep it, it's yours now. Every kid needs a basketball."

Frankie looked up at Simon.

Simon said, "Robert said you can keep it forever. He gave you a basketball. Wasn't that nice of him?"

261

Frankie wrapped his arms around the ball, holding it close, his eyes on Robert. "Thank you, sir."

"Don't call me sir. Want to see something cool?"

Frankie nodded. "Yes, please."

Robert floated three feet up in the air. "I can fly. What do you think about that?"

Frankie's jaw dropped. "Like a bird?"

"Better than a bird, way faster. I can teach you if you want."

Frankie looked at Clara.

Clara said, "That sounds like so much fun! You should let Robert teach you how to fly, but only if you want to."

Frankie smiled. "Yes, please. I want to fly."

Robert took Frankie's hand in his, the two of them floating up into the air, Frankie letting out a shriek. "I'm flying! I'm a bird!"

They floated back down, Frankie running back to Simon. "I was flying!"

"I know you were, that was amazing, the coolest thing ever."

A woman with long dark hair and a striking purple swimsuit appeared in a blink of light next to Robert, smiling at Simon and Clara.

Robert said, "This is Dorothy, she's my therapist."

Dorothy laughed. "But mostly his girlfriend. You

must be Simon and Clara. Robert has told me so much about you. He said you were instrumental in resolving certain issues with his former wife Bertha. I thank you for that."

"We were glad to help."

Dorothy kneeled down in front of Frankie, studying his face. "You miss your mama, don't you?"

Frankie nodded.

She rubbed the top of his head. "Want to know a secret?"

"Yes, please."

"Robert and I can help you find your mama. It will take a little while, but we can find her. You'd have to come with us though, leave Simon and Clara for a while. You can come back and visit them anytime you want to, the same way we came to visit you all the way from the beach in France."

Frankie looked up at Clara. "Can I go?"

"Of course you can. Robert and Dorothy can do a lot of things that Simon and I can't do. They can help you to find your mom."

Robert said, "First things first. Have you ever seen the Great Pyramid of Giza?"

Frankie shook his head. "Is it scary?"

"It's not scary at all, it's fun, we can sit on top, have a great view of the other pyramids. We'll probably see a camel. They have big humps on their back. They're goofy looking, walk funny. We can have lunch there. We can ride bikes in Paris. You'll like it, I'll get you a bicycle, a nice one. The food is great. Wonderful ambiance."

Dorothy laughed. "He's six, he doesn't know what ambiance is."

"We can teach him. Is he old enough to ride a bike?"

"If it's not too big for him. His feet have to reach the pedals."

Robert reached down and took Frankie's hand. "This is boring, let's go see the Great Pyramid. We can fly over the ocean, maybe see a whale swimming, ride on his back."

"Yes, sir."

"Don't call me sir, call me Robert."

Dorothy smiled, saying, "You two go ahead, I'll be there in a minute."

Frankie waved to Simon and Clara. "Bye."

"Bye, Frankie. Have lots of fun. Come back and visit whenever you want."

Robert and Frankie vanished in a blink of light.

Dorothy said, "Thank you so much for all you've done. Robert always wanted children, but never had any. This will be good for him, and good for me. I never had children either. I never seemed to have time, I was a psychotherapist who refused to take her own advice. It will take time for Frankie to understand that he died, and what that means, but once he does understand, we can reunite him with his mom."

"We like Robert a lot. I know he had a difficult life."

"I like him a lot too. I'd better get going before he asks Frankie if he wants to see a five-thousand-year-old mummy."

Clara laughed. "Come visit us anytime."

"We will." Dorothy gave a quick wave and vanished.

Simon rubbed his hands together. "Like I said, the best idea in the history of best ideas."

"You were right, the best idea ever. They're a family now."

"And, you'll be happy to know I made a momentous decision; I've decided just to relax and enjoy the rest of summer. How about we go for a nice boat ride in Ghost Lake?"

"How about we go see the ghost in the cemetery?"

# Chapter 22

"Simon, we don't have a choice, we have to talk to the ghost in the cemetery, there are no other ghosts on the estate. The only other ones we know are Robert, Frankie, and Dorothy, and they don't know anything about the murders."

"I'm not a fan of murderous rage filled ghosts. Suppose it pulls us into the ghost world, traps us there?"

"Sorry, did you just say 'pulls us into the ghost world?' How exactly would that happen? Can you explain the physics behind an event like that?"

"I was just speculating."

"We have to do it."

"I know we do, I know that, but I also feel like this is the appropriate time to procrastinate for as long as possible."

"Edward Briggs was scary, and that turned out fine. So will this, we'll be okay."

"It's been driving me crazy wondering who the ghost is. It has to be Cornelius, right?"

"It's not Cornelius, it's someone else, and I think you

know who."

Simon groaned. "Don't tell me, I don't want to know."

"Okay, I won't tell you, but only because you already know who it is, you just don't want to admit it. How about we do it Saturday morning?"

Simon nodded. "Daytime works best for me. No more nocturnal cemetery visits."

"Okay, enough about ghosts, let's do something fun, something without ghosts."

"Let's go for a swim in the lake, take the boat out. Splash around, dive into the water."

"That sounds fun. And there are no ghosts there to bother us."

"Exactly." Simon climbed into the truck, the two friends heading back toward Wilder House, Clara laughing about Robert wanting to show Frankie a mummy.

Simon said, "I want my mummy! Where's my mummy? Can you wake my mummy?"

Clara snorted. "That's awful, but kind of funny. I'm so glad they're a family now. Frankie will have so much fun."

"Robert's totally going to spoil him, get him ten bicycles, three motorcycles and a million toys."

"He doesn't actually buy the toys, he creates them with his mind, so it's not really spoiling him."

"It's totally spoiling him, it doesn't matter whether he

buys the toys or he creates them with his mind, he's still giving a–" Simon let out a screech, slamming on the brakes, the truck swerving wildly, tires squealing. Seconds later the truck lurched to a stop at the side of the road, Simon's knuckles white from gripping the wheel.

"What happened? Did you hit something?"

"I almost hit that guy!"

"What guy?"

"The guy in the road."

"There's no guy in the road, Simon."

Simon grabbed Clara's hand, a man appearing fifteen feet in front of the truck, his gaze directed at Simon and Clara.

"I see him, he's definitely a ghost."

"He's dressed in a brown uniform, wearing an old fashioned army helmet."

"Look at the medals on his chest, and the old rifle. He knows we can see him."

"Why is he looking at us?" Simon called out, "Hello? Can we help you?"

The soldier lowered his rifle, resting the butt of the weapon on the ground, holding the barrel with his left hand. He gave a smart salute with his right hand, holding it for almost five seconds, then lowered his hand. Before Simon could say anything, the man was gone, fading away to nothingness.

Simon's hands were still gripping the wheel. "Who was that? Why would we see a ghost soldier?"

"I don't know. It seemed like he knew us, but I have no idea who he was."

"He wasn't a sleeper, he knew exactly what he was doing."

"He saluted us, then vanished. Why would he do that?"

Simon shrugged, shaking his head. He put the truck into gear, heading down the highway. "Maybe he salutes everyone. You know what, there are way too many ghosts around here. I don't know how Edmund kept track of them all."

Simon turned into the long gravel driveway leading to Wilder House, parking his truck near the stone statue of Persephone, studying the blue car parked near the porch.

"That's Marion Jaggers' car. I wonder what she's doing here?"

The two friends headed inside, the sound of Marion's voice coming from a nearby room. Simon called out, "Mom?"

"We're in here!"

They stepped into the sitting room, Marion and Kate seated in a pair of comfortable armchairs.

"Marion has some good news for us."

"What kind of good news?"

269

Marion reached into her coat pocket, pulled out an Oreo cookie, brushed some lint off it, then offered it to Simon. "Cookie?"

"No, thanks, not really hungry."

She popped it into her mouth, holding up one finger, motioning for him to wait.

Simon gritted his teeth. She was doing it again, making them wait for the important news, like on those crazy reality shows.

Marion laughed, almost choking on the cookie. "Gets you every time. You should see the look on your face."

"What look?"

"Okay, here's the deal, the nutshell version. I know a guy who knows a guy, and it's all set up for the last two weeks in October."

"What's all set up for the last two weeks in October?"

"The show."

"What show?"

Marion grinned. "I thought you'd never ask. It's an art exhibition at the Scott Gallery in Manhattan, very prestigious institution, been there for over a hundred years."

"An exhibition of the new paintings we found in the basement?"

"Bingo, nail on the head. Bravo, young sir. Fireworks. Honorary degree."

Simon stared at Marion, uncertain what to make of

270

her response. Was she being funny? "Right. So, what kind of show is it, exactly?"

"The science fiction paintings you found in the basement will be on display for a month in Manhattan. The word is out about a newly discovered cache of paintings by Edmund Wilder hidden in the basement of Wilder House. It's going to be big. Lollapalooza big."

"Are we selling them?"

"Need to sell a few paintings to buy gas for your truck?"

"What? No, it's not that. I don't think we should sell them. I want to study them all, they're really cool."

Clara nodded her approval. "Simon is right, we should study them."

Marion's eyes narrowed. "I know when someone is up to something, and you two are up to your necks in it."

"What? We're not up to anything, we just like the paintings. They're different, really interesting. I didn't know he had such a great imagination."

"Kate already decided not to sell them, exhibition only, maybe sell prints. Nothing suspicious about you two. Totally up to something, in my bones, feeling it."

Simon attempted a disarming smile. "So, what's the gallery like? Is it nice?"

"Changing the topic, the old diversion ploy, I like it. You'd make a good lawyer. Scott Gallery is highly respected, best of the best, so on and so on, ad infinitum. And it's haunted, just like Ghost Lake."

Simon blinked. "It's haunted? Really? A haunted art gallery?"

"Not the gallery, per se, just one painting. There's a haunted painting. People have seen a ghostly blue form standing in front of the painting, just like the ghost I saw at the lake. It's been seen multiple times. Half a dozen night guards claim they've seen something, felt cold chills, two of them quit, freaked out."

"How could a painting be haunted?"

"How can anything be haunted? It's an 1884 painting of an old house. The story is that someone was brutally murdered in the house. They say–"

Kate held up her hand. "Please, no more ghost stories, I won't sleep tonight. I don't want to know about some dreadful murder."

Marion pulled another cookie from her pocket. "Up to something. Both of you. So transparent."

"The only thing we're up to is going for a relaxing swim in the lake on a beautiful sunny summer day."

Clara nodded. "It's so nice out."

Marion shrugged. "I'll let it go for now, but I expect to see you both at the exhibition. People will go nuts, Edmund's living relatives, are you kidding? Emma Weatherby's granddaughter? Bring a pen, you'll be signing autographs, giving speeches, lots of photographs."

Simon panicked. "What? I'm not giving a speech, that's not going to happen."

Marion snorted, slapping the table. "Gets them every time. Speeches, am I right? They're the worst; giving them *and* listening to them. The worst. You two lovebirds go have your swim while Kate and I hash out the details of the show."

Simon and Clara exited the sitting room, stepping out onto the porch, Simon leaning over and whispering, "Does she know something? About the ghosts? Why would she tell us about the haunted painting?"

"I don't think she knows, but it's pretty obvious to her that we're hiding something. She's a lawyer, she knows how to read people. We'll have to be careful."

"Let's go for a swim."

"I think we're forgetting something."

"Like what?"

"Our swim suits?"

"Oh, right. I'll drive you home and you can get yours."

"Or we could just go for a boat ride. You could row me around the lake, serenade me with romantic songs, give me a big lithographed box of chocolates."

"Trust me, you don't want to hear me sing."

"Or we could go talk to the ghost in the cemetery."

Simon's smile vanished. "What?"

"We're both here, why wait?"

Simon's eyes narrowed. "You tricked me, didn't you? You lured me here under the pretext of a fun relaxing swim in the lake, knowing full well we were actually going to talk to the cemetery ghost."

"Marion was right, you'd make an excellent lawyer."

Simon gazed at the dense forest for moment, then said, "I guess there's no point in putting it off. I have to know who it is. I have to. Even if it is some hideous spectral phantasm who wants to pull us into the ghost world."

"No more scary movies for you. Let's go."

They headed down the hill toward the lake, Simon pointing to a narrow path through the dense pine trees. "That way."

Clara swatted at a buzzing fly. "The flies are bad."

Ten minutes later they stepped into the clearing, Simon eyeing the rows of gravestones. "Cemeteries are so creepy."

"Agnes said the unmarked grave is beyond the cemetery, but she didn't say how far beyond."

"I guess we look for a mound of dirt or something, maybe a pile of rocks."

"Or you could put your ring on and look for an angry spectral phantasm."

"Let's find the grave first, then put the ring on. I don't like surprises."

They pressed on through the pine trees, Simon scanning the ground for anything resembling an old grave.

It was Clara who spotted it when she stepped into a small clearing. "There, that has to be it."

Simon eyed the two sticks that had been tied together with coarse twine to form a crude cross. "Why would they do that? Why put the cross there?"

Clara furrowed her brow. "Maybe whoever murdered him felt guilty, wanted to do something to make themselves feel better."

"That makes sense, but it's also seriously creepy." Simon shivered. "I'm cold."

"Me too. Really cold."

"It's here, isn't it?"

Clara nodded. "It's not an it, it's a who."

"The final resting place of Police Chief Walter Merrick."

"Except we both know he's not resting."

Simon groaned, stepping back from the grave, his back pressed against the thick pine trees. Clara stood next to him, taking his hand.

"Are you ready to do this?"

"No, but let's do it anyway."

"Just another day in the life of two lovebird

paranormal investigators."

Simon laughed, reaching into his pocket for the ghost ring. He took a deep breath, then slipped it onto his finger.

# Chapter 23

Simon instinctively jumped back when he saw it, a deep visceral fear rolling through him, the sharp pine needles jabbing into his back. Clara stood silently, her eyes on the roiling amorphous black shape hovering above the grave, thin red glowing filaments swirling and twisting in and out of the cloud, sometimes blurred, sometimes sharply in focus.

Simon whispered, "Holy crap, that thing is terrifying, so scary. I don't want to get near it. What are those red things? I've never seen that before."

"Simon, maybe you're right, maybe we shouldn't be doing this. There's something off about this. Something dark, something..."

"I believe the word you're desperately searching for is evil?"

"Maybe, I don't know. Agnes was right about the anger, the rage."

Simon was remembering Tobias Granger's memory of Chief Merrick, his blotchy suspicious face staring at him through the open doorway. "Chief Merrick was a horrible person, but he was a person, not a spectral demon who wants to pull us into the ghost world."

"Again, not something that happens."

"I know that, I'm just saying he was a person like everyone else in the world. Just a super vengeful murderous one who would drag us into the ghost world if that was a thing. He started out as a child. A kid, like Frankie."

"That makes me feel a little better, except for the murderous rage part. I know what you're saying though. Our imagined fears are almost always worse than the reality."

"Exactly. Which is why we should probably go for a nice swim in the lake instead of touching this evil nightmare who wants to pull us into the ghost world."

"You said it, he's not a demon, he's a person."

Simon groaned. "Enough procrastinating, let's do it. I have to know."

They stepped closer to the black swirling maelstrom, a low roaring sound filling Simon's ears. "Do you hear that?"

Clara nodded. "It sounds like waves crashing."

"Crashing waves that want to murder you."

"Stop."

"Okay, I'll count to three, then, and only then, after I say three, I will, without hesitation, and with minimal trepidation, reach out with either my left arm, or possibly my right arm, extending my hand, or maybe–"

Clara stuck her hand into the horrifying black

miasma, the red swirling threads winding around her fingers.

The forest was gone, Simon sitting in inky blackness, his eyes gradually becoming accustomed to the dark. "Clara?"

"I'm here. I'm sitting on a bed. I'm so sad, it's awful. And I'm scared. I am so scared, Simon."

"I know, I feel sick." Simon looked down at the ragged clothes he was wearing. "I'm a kid." He looked at his hands. "About six years old, like Frankie."

"Why is he sitting alone in a dark little room?"

Simon heard a boy's thin wavering voice call out. "I'll be good, I promise."

There was an empty silence.

Simon looked at his bare arms. "He has bruises on his arms. Bad ones."

"He's being punished, beaten, locked in a dark room."

Simon was shaking. This was not good, not good at all. He jumped when he heard the sound of a key turning, a loud click, the doorknob twisting, a crack of light appearing, the door opening slowly, Simon staring in horror at the unshaven old man wearing filthy coveralls, no shirt, a whiskey bottle in one hand, bloodshot eyes, his face cruel and twisted. "Say you're sorry, boy. Say it so I believe it."

"I'm sorry, Mister Craven, I'm sorry I broke it. I

279

didn't mean to, I was just–"

The door slammed shut, the key clicking, Simon and Clara in a cloud of swirling darkness, filled with a terrible unfathomable fear.

The room vanished, Simon sprinting through a dark alley, adrenaline pumping through his body, his heart pounding. Someone was chasing him, shouting. He heard a police whistle blow.

"He's in the alley, block the other end! He can't get out!"

Simon looked down at his body. He was older, stronger, sixteen or seventeen. He was holding a fistful of cash. He stuffed it into his pocket, searching the alley for a way out, spotting a metal fire escape. He leaped up, grabbing the bottom rung, pulling himself up, racing up the metal stairs, reaching the roof. He stopped to peer down from the roof, spotting three policemen in the alley, their guns drawn. "Where is he? Where did he go?"

Walter raced across the rooftop, Simon giving a yelp when he realized what was going to happen. Walter was going to leap across a gap between two four-story buildings.

Clara cried out, "He's going to jump!"

Simon didn't look down as he leaped over the ten-foot-wide chasm, rolling onto the neighboring roof, smashing his shoulder against a brick chimney.

He staggered to his feet, running ahead, leaping across to the next rooftop, heading down the fire escape, peering into the apartment windows. One of them was open, he clambered inside, a man jumping up from a kitchen table, grabbing a long knife, backing away. Simon raced across the room, yanking the door open, stepping into a long hallway. Ten minutes later he was walking down a crowded city street, his hand pressing against the wad of cash in his pocket.

He reached a narrow alleyway, spotting a man in a black coat leaning back against the brick wall, a lit cigarette dangling from his mouth. The man looked up at him. "You did it?"

Simon approached the man, pulling the cash from his pocket. "Just like I said."

"Coppers?"

"Flatfoots, I seen turtles run faster."

The man laughed, handing Walter a twenty dollar bill. "Good job, sonny boy. Monk said to give you this, said to hide it somewhere good. Might need it." He reached into his pocket, pulling out a black short-barreled revolver, handing it to Walter.

Walter eyed the gun, flipping open the cylinder, spinning it, then snapping it shut in a single motion, stuffing the gun into his coat pocket. "Thanks."

"Don't kill nobody without Monk say so."

Walter nodded. "Got it, don't kill nobody."

"Unless you got to."

"I got a list."

The man in the black coat laughed. Walter did not.

Clara whispered, "He has a list of people he wants to kill?"

"Probably the man who locked him in the room. Maybe he's just trying to sound tough."

"We could end this, we could leave if it gets too bad."

"We need to find out what happened, solve the other two murders."

"Other three murders. Walter was murdered too, buried in the unmarked grave."

Walter's memory swirled darkly, Simon and Clara returning to brilliant daylight. They were sitting in an old car, a man leaning in through the window, handing Walter a wad of cash.

"Monk knows you was the one what shot him. You need to make yourself scarce, go somewhere, lay low. He ain't a guy what lets it go."

Walter nodded. "I'll get that snake next time. Or someone else will."

He turned the key, the old car starting, then engine coughing. An hour later he had left Brooklyn behind him, on his way to somewhere far away, some place no one ever heard of, a place called Caligo Falls in upstate New

Hampshire. Just him and the squirrels until Monk wasn't a problem.

Clara whispered, "He tried to kill Monk, his boss."

"And now Monk is after him."

The memory flashed forward, Simon finding himself standing outside of Wilder House talking to Cornelius Wilder. Cornelius was studying Walter's face, gauging his expression. "I hear you're a man who knows how to do what needs to be done."

Walter shrugged. "I'm your guy. Do whatever you want for a price. Don't matter what."

"I have a better idea. How would you like go legit, be a police chief?"

Walter snorted. "You're dreaming. I ain't a copper."

"You could be. I could arrange it, make a big donation to your election, make one to the Caligo Falls City Council, recommend you, say you used to be a big cop in New York. They won't check, they just want a new police chief, they don't care where he's from. You can help me a lot more as the police chief, and it would all be legal."

"For real?"

"For real. And you'd still get paid for doing what needs to be done."

Walter laughed. "Never thought I'd see the day, me a copper."

Clara said, "Walter was working for Cornelius."

The scene changed again, Simon now in the first floor sitting room, Cornelius leaning forward, his voice low.

"There's a matter that needs to be attended to. An old partner of mine is coming to Wilder House. I asked him to come, told him I wanted to make things right, maybe a merger between our two rail lines. He's been gathering information about me, about my business dealings. He's going to blackmail me, try to get his oil shipping contract back. That can't happen."

"So he never makes it back to New York?"

"It can't be connected to me, it has to be someone else."

"A patsy. I can do that. I got just the guy. He's been drunk and disorderly more times than I can count."

"You're talking about Josiah Finch?"

"That's the one, everyone knows he's nothing but a stinking drunk. So he blacks out, does the deed, then tops himself. Done and done. Even better, I'll be the guy that saw him do it."

"That works. I'll get Frederick drunk, promise him everything, then you pick him up and take him to the train station."

Simon said, "I knew it, Cornelius was behind Frederick's murder."

It was suddenly nighttime, Simon seated behind the wheel of the police car, Walter glancing over at a drunken

Frederick Thornton. He was slumped over, snoring, drool coming from his mouth, his jaw slack, his jacket hanging open. It was the first time Simon and Clara could hear Walter's thoughts.

"Stinkin' drunk. You got no idea what's going to happen, do you. Won't be long now and you'll be singin' with the angels, more likely the devil."

Simon could see the entrance to the gravel driveway that led to Josiah's house. Walter slowed the car down, stopping in the middle of the road. There would be no other cars at this time of night.

Frederick snorted loudly, sitting up, his bloodshot eyes trying to focus on the road. "What? We there?"

"Not yet, sir. I have to put some water in the radiator, it's overheating, one of the hoses is leaking."

Frederick's head slumped down again, mumbling something to himself.

Walter shut off the headlights, leaving the overhead cab light on, climbing out of the police car, pulling out a heavy revolver from under the car seat. He strolled forward twenty feet, then stopped, turning toward the car. He could see Frederick looking at him, squinting his eyes, trying to focus.

It was over before Simon knew what was happening, Walter firing three bullets through the windshield. He heard a groan, Frederick falling forward, his head hitting the dashboard.

"It was Merrick who shot Thornton."

"And Cornelius paid him to do it."

Walter put the gun back in his pocket, climbing into the car. He reached over to Frederick, checking for a pulse. There was none.

"Hey, buddy, did you see that? You just got shot by Josiah Finch. Let's go pay him a visit, make him pay for what he done."

Walter put the car in gear, turning down the driveway, coming to a stop when he reached Josiah's house. He shut off the lights, climbing out of the car, stepping over to a window, peering inside.

"Drunk again, what a surprise."

He pulled the revolver from his pocket, gingerly turning the doorknob, inching the front door open, stepping into the house. He walked silently over to the bed, studying Josiah for a moment. "Nighty-night, pal."

He fired one shot, then wrapped Josiah's lifeless fingers around the pistol grip, dropping it on the bed next to him. He looked around the room, spotting an empty whiskey bottle. "That works." He picked it up, setting it next to Josiah. "Just couldn't live with what you done. Ain't that sad."

Simon felt sick. "He just shot him. He was sleeping and Merrick shot him. Who could do that, then make a joke about it?"

"I don't know. He's sick, or evil, or both."

Merrick's voice sounded in their thoughts.

"He was drunken garbage, just like Craven. "

"You can hear us?"

"Who are you, how are you in my head?"

"We're reliving your memories."

"This is a memory?"

"It is. You murdered Frederick Thornton and Josiah Finch."

"I did what had to be done. That's how it works."

Clara said, "Who is Craven?"

"He ain't nobody now. I went back and did what had to be done."

"He was the man who put you in the dark room?"

"I put him in a dark room only he ain't coming out."

"What about Tobias Granger? Do you remember what happened to him?"

"I remember. What a sucker that guy was."

Simon found himself standing in a dark corner of the basement, his eyes on the second closet door, watching as Cornelius and Tobias stepped into the tunnel. He could hear Cornelius telling Tobias he needed some crates of whiskey moved, put on the shelves in the secret room.

"You were there the whole time, hiding in the basement."

"The chauffeur had to go. He was listening when me and Mr. Wilder were talking about what happened to Thornton. Mr. Wilder was laughing about it, saying he wasn't going to pay me for the three bullets I used. Joking about the threats that Thornton made to him. Saying he won't be making no more threats to nobody. We were drinking. I heard something at the door, snuck over and opened it, caught that weasel Tobias listening to us. He must have heard everything. We had to make sure he never told nobody. Just how it works."

Walter waited until he saw Cornelius leave the room and head up the stairs. He pulled a revolver from his pocket, spinning the cylinder, making sure it was loaded. Cornelius wanted him to use this gun, who knows why. He crept forward, entering the tunnel, peering into the secret room, waiting until Tobias was done moving the whiskey crates. Tobias had his back to Walter, he was looking at the crates of whiskey, rubbing his shoulder.

Walter stepped out and raised the pistol, firing once. Tobias groaned, looking down at his chest. Walter fired again, Tobias falling to the floor, motionless.

"You killed Tobias."

"A loose end that Mr. Wilder wanted tied up. He knew about us killing Thornton."

"He didn't know. He was outside the room but he didn't hear anything. It was muffled, he was telling the truth."

Walter shrugged. "Either way he ain't talking. Just taking out the trash. Mr. Wilder will tell everyone the chauffeur went to work for some big guy in Chicago, paid him twice what Cornelius was paying him. Complained about it, pretended he was mad at him, then said he understood why he done it. All about the money. They all believed him. We cleared all the whiskey out and locked up the tunnel."

"What about you? What happened to you?"

# Chapter 24

"What happened to me? Nothing happened to me, we got away with it. Mr. Wilder always gets away with it."

"You don't remember anything? About what happened behind the little cemetery?"

Simon felt like the air was being sucked out of the room, a terrible darkness creeping inside him, his insides twisting. Clara gasped, "Simon, what's happening?"

"That roaring sound, it's getting louder!"

The world seemed to turn red, then black, a terrible shrieking rage filling Simon, the roaring almost unbearable. "I think he's remembering!"

"I can see those red things, they're swirling around me. What are they?"

"Should we go?"

"Not yet, we have to see what happened to him."

There was a sudden shocking eerie silence, Simon striding across the covered porch of Wilder House. He pushed open the front door without knocking, the butler stepping out of the sitting room, giving him a disapproving look.

"You are here to see Mr. Wilder, I presume?"

"You presume right. Where is he?"

"Mr. Wilder would prefer it if all visitors knocked on the front door before entering, whereupon I should answer the door, cordially greeting whoever it might be."

"I ain't all visitors, I'm the Police Chief. Where is he?"

"Of course, sir, my mistake, right this way."

Walter followed the butler to one of the first floor studies, the butler knocking on the door, then opening it. Cornelius was sitting at a desk sifting through a stack of papers. "What is it?"

"Police Chief Merrick is here to see you, sir. He was quite insistent."

"Send him in."

The butler motioned for Walter to enter the room.

Cornelius looked up at Merrick. "What is it?"

"What is it? I need to get paid more, that's what is it."

"Paid more for what? You have received ample remuneration for all the work you've done."

"Not enough. I'd get way more if I was back with the Eastman Gang in Brooklyn."

"You'd be dead, you tried to kill Monk Eastman. Bad idea. They're still looking for you."

"I need to get paid more. I know stuff."

Cornelius's eyes turned to ice. "Are you threatening me?"

"No, just saying we're partners in a lot of stuff, and we should share the profits."

Cornelius shrugged, setting his pen down. "Fair enough, I suppose. You have done a lot for me. Tied up some loose ends."

"You know it."

"How about a five thousand dollar bonus and you help me dig up a strongbox I buried back by the old cemetery?" He reached into a drawer, pulling out an envelope filled with hundred dollar bills, tossing it onto the desk in front of Walter. "Five thousand, as agreed."

Walter grabbed the money, stuffing it into his coat pocket. "That's more like it. We're back in business, boss."

Cornelius laughed. "Worth every penny. Do you have time to help me dig up the strongbox? I buried it two years ago, almost forgot about it. Over fifty thousand in cash, I won't tell you how I got it. How about an extra five hundred to help? Probably best if I don't ask the gardener to dig it up."

Merrick laughed. "You got it. For five hundred bucks I can do it right now."

Cornelius stood up, grabbing his coat, heading out of the study, Merrick walking behind him.

They walked out onto the porch, Cornelius saying, "You have an election coming up. How is it looking?

Any competition? You need a campaign donation?"

"Nobody else running. Guess I scared them all away."

"Good to hear."

They stopped at the gardener's shack, Walter grabbing a long handled shovel. "Been a long time since I used one of these, back in the early days in Brooklyn. Don't miss it one bit. I'd go back and kill that bastard Craven again if I could. He won't be locking nobody in a room anytime soon. "

"Understandable. He got what he deserved. You've come a long way since then."

"Damn right I did." He reached into his pocket, his hand pressing against the stack of hundred dollar bills.

The two men made their way through the dense pine forest, Cornelius the first to step into the small cemetery. Merrick eyed the rows of gravestones, laughing. "Friends of yours, guys what crossed you?"

Cornelius laughed. "No, they died from the Spanish Flu, household servants mostly, a few of their children. A lot of people died."

"Happens to us all."

"Sad but true, I'm afraid. The strongbox is about twenty paces back from here."

Cornelius pushed through the trees, taking measured steps, counting them out loud. They reached a small clearing, Cornelius stopping. "Here we are, weeds have grown up, not certain where it is. Just start digging there, and keep going toward that tree until you hit it. It's only a foot or two down. The ground should be soft."

Half an hour later, Merrick was sweating profusely, staring at the six-foot-long hole he'd dug. He wiped his forehead on his sleeve. "You sure this is the right place? Almost two feet down and there's nothing, no box."

"Look, down there, is that it?"

Merrick leaned over the hole, peering down at the rich forest soil. "Where? I don't see nothing."

"Nobody threatens me. Nobody."

Walter turned around, his eyes widening when he saw the black revolver in Cornelius' hand.

"What's that for? What are you doing?"

"Nobody threatens me, especially not some lowlife gutter trash who's gotten way too big for his britches."

"I didn't threaten you, boss, I just thought–"

Cornelius fired three times, the roar of the gun muffled by the dense pine forest. Walter spun around, tumbling to the ground, blood spreading out across his shirt.

Cornelius put the gun back in his coat pocket, stepping over Walter's lifeless body, plucking the envelope of cash from his pocket. "You won't be needing this where you're going."

He rolled Walter into the grave, using the shovel to fill it in, spreading leaves and pine needles over the

294

freshly dug earth.

"Nobody threatens me. Nobody."

They were back in the clearing again, the whirling black miasma gone, a ghostly man dressed in an old fashioned police uniform standing in front of them. His eyes were on the small wooden cross.

"He killed me! After everything I done, he shot me dead. I will murder him! I swear on my grave I will find him and kill him. He is a dead man!"

Simon said, "Cornelius died long ago, in 1958. He's gone, not here anymore, he's dead."

"It's 1925, moron."

"No, you were murdered by Cornelius a hundred years ago. You've been sleeping, time has passed. You're waking up now."

"A hundred years ago? I don't get it, who are you?"

"I'm Simon Moody, and this is my friend Clara Barley. Cornelius Wilder was my great uncle, Edmund Wilder's grandfather. We can see people who have died, we relive their memories."

"I'm a ghost?"

"You're still you, just without a physical body."

"He murdered me. He has to pay for it."

Clara said, "He already has."

"What do I do? I never been dead before. Where is everyone? Where's Mr. Wilder?"

"They all moved on to what comes next."

"What is it? What comes next?"

"I don't know, I just know they go somewhere else."

Simon and Clara jumped back when the shimmering blue form appeared, a rotund man wearing an expensive three piece suit, a gold watch chain dangling from his vest pocket.

Clara stared in stunned surprise at the last person she had expected to see. It was the ghost of Cornelius Wilder. He floated over to Walter, stopping in front of him.

"Hello, Walter."

"You! I will kill you!" He lunged forward, trying to grab Cornelius by the throat, his hands passing through him. "What is this? What are you?"

"I'm a ghost, just like you. We're both dead now, both of us. We were misguided fools, and now we're dead. We wasted our lives. I can show you everything, teach you, if you want that."

"You murdered me."

"I did, and I paid a high price for it. I have come to understand a great many things since that day. I can teach you, it is my only redemption."

"Teach me what?"

"Come with me." Cornelius held out his hand.

"You murdered me. After everything I did for you."

"After everything you did for yourself, and after

296

everything I did for myself. We never did anything for anyone else."

Walter looked over to Simon and Clara. "What should I do? I can't kill him, he's dead."

"Go with him. He's not the same person you knew."

Walter turned his gaze to Cornelius. "Is it better there?"

Cornelius nodded. "You can see everything. No one will hurt you. No one will lock you in a room."

Walter reached out and took Cornelius' hand, the two men vanishing in a blink of light.

Simon could hardly speak, his eyes on Clara. "I don't believe it. Cornelius killed Merrick."

"And Merrick spent the last hundred years filled with a blinding rage, not knowing where he was, seeking revenge against Cornelius."

"What happened to Cornelius? Why did he come back for Merrick?"

"He said it was his only redemption, to help the person he had murdered."

"I was not expecting that. I was not expecting any of this. Was Merrick evil? Was Cornelius evil?"

"Cornelius said it himself, they were misguided. Merrick was angry at life, filled with rage at the world he was born into, at Craven, the man who locked him in the little room."

"He had those bruises all over his arms. Craven probably got drunk and beat Walter. That's why he was the way he was, why he hated drunks. It's weird that he hated drunks but he drank more than anyone."

"And he probably hated himself for doing it. None of that excuses the horrific things he did, the people he killed. He made his own choices, lived his life the way he wanted to. Not everyone who is abused as a child becomes a murderer."

"It's sad though."

"There's nothing sadder."

Clara put her arms around Simon, holding him close. "I'm glad I met you."

"I can't imagine not knowing you."

They held each other for a long time.

"We should go back."

"There are no ghosts left. They're gone, all of them."

"Except for the ghost soldier who stopped us on the road."

"He probably salutes everyone, a classic example of the saluting ghost syndrome."

"That's not a thing. Let's head back. We still have time to go swimming."

"We could just row around the lake."

"Are you going to serenade me?"

"That might scare the fish. How about if I play music

298

on my phone?"

"Romantic music?"

"That works."

Clara stepped away from Simon. "Wait, let's not do that. I have a better idea."

"What could be better than rowing around the lake listening to music?"

"Only the best idea in the history of best ideas in the known universe."

"That sounds very familiar, almost like something I said."

"It's exactly like something you said. It's also a secret, just like your best idea in the history of best ideas. Get your truck keys, we're going for a little ride, cowboy."

# Chapter 25

Simon and Clara headed back through the forest, making their way around the house to the gardens, stopping when they saw Harrington clipping spent blossoms off a lovely flowering tree. He set his clippers down and waved. "You two have been rather busy the last few weeks. Dare I ask what has been occupying your time?"

Simon held up the ghost ring. "This has. It's a long story, but we've been helping spirits move on."

"You've been to the old cemetery?"

"We have. Why?"

"Just idle curiosity. I have set flowers there on occasion and gotten quite an alarming chill."

"You won't be getting that chill anymore."

"Wonderful. The Shadow Ring is in good hands, as I knew it would be. Perhaps when you have completed your self-appointed tasks you would be kind enough to recount the details of your latest adventure to me. Edmund would be extremely proud of you."

Clara's eyes were focused on the purple flowering tree. "We'd love to tell you everything, but it's going to be a few days until we're finished. The flowers on that tree are beautiful, they almost glow in the sunlight, and they smell incredible."

Simon said, "What kind of flowers are they? Where is the tree from? Is it native to New Hampshire?"

Harrington smiled. "And there it is, an encapsulation of the great human dichotomy."

Simon gave a puzzled look. "What great dichotomy?"

"Whether to feel the world, to wordlessly experience it with our senses, as Clara just did with the purple flowers, or to categorize it and analyze it, as you just did with your three questions. An artist would look at these lovely blossoms and see one thing, a botanist would see something else entirely."

Simon stared at the tree. "Can't you do both? Switch back and forth?"

Harrington smiled. "Excellent. I look forward to hearing all about your exploits in the spectral world."

Simon and Clara made their way to the parking area, Simon saying, "Where are we going?"

"Top secret, need to know only. Sorry."

Soon they were driving down the gravel drive to the highway.

"Which way do I turn?"

"Head toward the town center."

"Are we going to see Robert, is it something about Frankie?"

"That was your greatest idea in the world, not mine. I'll tell you when to turn."

As they were approaching the town center, Clara called out, "Turn left! There!"

Simon hit the brakes, taking a sharp turn, the wheels squealing.

"A heads up would be nice. Where are we going?"

"Turn right!"

"At the police station?"

"I need to report a murder."

"We're really doing this?"

"We are. We're going to prove definitively that Josiah Finch was innocent, that he was framed for the murder of Frederick Thornton. Then we're going to tell Bobby Finch."

"That is absolutely, beyond a shadow of a doubt, the second greatest idea in the history of great ideas."

Clara rolled her eyes. "Let's go."

The two friends stepped into the police station, spotting Sergeant Rogers. He was talking on the phone, but motioned for them to sit. "I see, the issue has been resolved? Excellent, and no injuries? A tragedy averted. Glad to hear it, have a great day."

He hung up the phone, eyeing Simon and Clara. "Mrs. Beasley's dog Tusker chased the neighbor's cat up a tree again, but she lured him down with snacks."

Simon grinned. "We have something a little more interesting than that."

Clara said, "I want to report a murder."

"What?"

Simon added, "Four murders, we want to report four murders."

"False reporting of a crime is a serious offense."

"There's a skeleton in the basement of Wilder House. He was shot twice and we know who he was, a man named Tobias Granger, Cornelius Wilder's bodyguard. There's also a murder victim buried behind a small cemetery near Wilder House. We think it's Walter Merrick, murdered by Cornelius Wilder, and we think we have the gun that shot both of them. And the bullets."

Sergeant Rogers stared at them silently.

Clara added, "In 1923, Police Chief Walter Merrick allegedly witnessed the murder of Cornelius Wilder's partner, Frederick Thornton. He testified in court that he had seen Josiah Finch shoot Frederick Thornton. He was lying, Chief Merrick shot and killed both of them, Finch and Thornton."

Sergeant Rogers leaned back in his chair, drumming his fingers on the desk. "Does this have anything to do with ghosts?"

Clara shook her head. "It has nothing to do with ghosts, and everything to do with hard evidence."

303

Simon said, "Is it possible you still have the gun that Josiah Finch supposedly used to end his own life? It could be checked for fingerprints, DNA. Merrick testified under oath that he had witnessed the crime, so I doubt the gun was ever checked for fingerprints. And there was no DNA testing back then to prove him wrong."

"This has something to do with the old police car?"

"It does. The car could also be checked for trace evidence, maybe DNA from the blood on the front seat."

Sergeant Rogers sat up straight, rubbing his hands together. "Just like the old days in Chicago. Who doesn't love a good cold case? We have an offsite evidence locker that goes way back, and we keep everything."

Two days later, Mrs. Morley was looking out the kitchen window when she saw a police car pull into the parking area. "Oh, good heavens, what have they done now? I hope they're not in trouble."

It was Harrington who answered the knock on the door.

"Good afternoon, officer. How may I help you?"

"I'm Sergeant Rogers of the Caligo Falls Police Department, here to see Simon Moody and Clara Barley."

"They are waiting for you upstairs in the second floor sitting area. Follow me if you would."

Sergeant Rogers made his way up the grand staircase,

eyeing the large portraits on the wall. He pointed to one of them. "That's Cornelius Wilder?"

"Quite correct, sir. He was Edmund Wilder's grandfather."

"I see."

They stepped up to the second floor, Simon and Clara standing next to the open wall safe. "It's in here."

Sergeant Rogers stepped over to the safe, shining a small flashlight onto the old revolver and the box of bullets. "An old Colt Model 1917, military issue. You don't see many of those around. Did you touch it?"

Simon shook his head. "I looked at it, but I didn't leave any fingerprints. I was careful."

"This is the gun you think killed Tobias Granger, the skeleton you found in the basement?"

"Yes, we believe Chief Merrick used it to murder Cornelius Wilder's chauffeur, Tobias Granger."

"Why did he do it?"

Clara said, "We don't know exactly why, but the bullets should match the ones we found with the body in the secret tunnel."

"And you think Cornelius used this same gun to murder Chief Merrick?"

"We think the bullets will match the ones you'll find near the body of Chief Merrick, buried behind the old cemetery in the woods."

"Leave the gun here, don't touch anything. I'm calling in a team of forensic specialists from Manchester, all the latest high tech equipment, ground scanners, DNA, the works. They'll be checking everything, including the old police car at Billy Whitaker's car museum. Did you touch the skeleton in the basement?"

"No, but we did use a metal detector to find two bullets near the skeleton. I put them in this plastic bag, but I didn't touch them. I can show you exactly where we found them." She handed the bullets to Sergeant Rogers.

"Excellent. Forensic investigators should arrive tomorrow. Just to reiterate, this has nothing to do with ghosts?"

"The evidence will speak for itself."

"You didn't answer my question. How did you know about the unmarked grave behind the cemetery, who was buried there?"

Simon did something he had always wanted to do. He gave an enigmatic smile.

Sergeant Rogers pursed his lips. "Never mind, I don't want to know. I'll say you stumbled onto it when you were searching the area with a metal detector, saw the cross, thought it looked like an old grave. We can identify the body using DNA. Oh, it took a while, but I found the gun that Josiah Finch allegedly used to take his own life, and the three bullets that killed Frederick Thornton, recovered from his body at the time of the murder. It was in the offsite evidence locker, stacks of dusty old boxes, just like in the movies. Nothing digitized, just good old fashioned tedious police work."

Simon laughed. "Nice."

There was a flurry of activity at Wilder House for the next two days, a very anxious Mrs. Morley peering out the window at the group of crime scene investigators emerging from the forest. "Oh, great heavens! Is that a body bag? What have Simon and Clara gotten themselves into?"

Simon opened the kitchen door an hour later, saying, "You can come out now, Mrs. Morley, they took the skeleton from the basement. It's gone."

Mrs. Morley shivered. "All these years with that dreadful skeleton right below us. Thank goodness it's gone. You're not in any kind of trouble are you? You and Clara?"

"No trouble at all, I think we solved four murders, we might even be heroes."

"Don't tell me, I don't want to know anything about it, murders at Wilder House, Edmund would not have liked this at all. Would either of you care for a lovely piece of chocolate cake?"

Simon was about to say he would kill for one, then wisely decided not to. The most important part of making hilarious jokes was knowing when not to make them.

"That sounds great, thanks Mrs. Morley."

Exactly two weeks later, and two weeks before Simon and Clara headed off to college, there was a knock on the front door, Harrington answering it.

"Sergeant Rogers, how nice to see you. Please come in, everyone is waiting for you."

They met in the first floor sitting room, Sergeant Rogers taking a seat in a comfortable armchair, Simon, Clara, Kate, Harrington, and Marion Jaggers waiting for him to speak.

"Simon and Clara, you were right about everything. The gun found with Josiah Finch was the same gun used to kill Frederick Thornton. We found Finch and Merrick's fingerprints and DNA on the gun, but the key bits of evidence were the bullets in the gun. The only fingerprints on them were those of Chief Merrick, which meant he was the one who loaded the gun that killed Frederick and Josiah. His fingerprints were also on the whiskey bottle found on the bed next to Josiah. We did a background check on Chief Merrick, something which surprisingly had not been done before he was elected. It turns out he was once a member of the Eastman Gang, an organized criminal group started in 1906 by a man named Monk Eastman. We found his fingerprints on old police records from back in the day. He had been a suspect in three or four murders but was never convicted, then he just disappeared.

"The skeleton in the basement was that of Tobias Granger, Cornelius Wilder's chauffeur, murdered for unknown reasons by Chief Merrick. The bullets you found near him were fired from the gun in the wall safe, the gun belonging to Cornelius Wilder, the gun that also killed Chief Merrick. There is strong circumstantial evidence for us to suspect that Chief Walter Merrick was murdered by Cornelius Wilder. We were unable to find any concrete evidence that Cornelius Wilder had ever purchased a house for Chief Merrick in California, or that Merrick had ever lived there. We believe that story was Cornelius Wilder's way of explaining away Chief Merrick's sudden disappearance."

Kate's jaw was hanging open. "Edmund's grandfather was a murderer?"

Sergeant Rogers nodded. "We are quite certain that he killed Chief Merrick to keep him quiet. Simon and Clara were right about everything. A forewarning, Wilder House is going to be in the news again. The Caligo Falls Gazette is planning to publish a story about the murders, and more than likely the story will be picked up by national news syndicates."

Kate frowned. "I can't even imagine what people will be saying about Wilder House now, the ghosts, the murders, and who knows what else."

Sergeant Rogers turned to Simon and Clara, raising his eyebrows. "Is that true, there are ghosts in Wilder House?"

Simon said, "I can say with one hundred percent certainty that there are currently no ghosts to be found in Wilder House."

"Currently?"

Simon gave his enigmatic smile.

Marion stood up, pulling her phone from her purse. "How about a photo to celebrate, one for the memory books. You can frame it, put it on your wall, just you and Clara. You done good, kiddos."

Simon shrugged. "I guess a photo would be okay."

Clara grinned, sliding over next to Simon.

Marion held up her phone, then lowered it. "Arms around each others shoulders, act like lovebirds."

"What?"

Mrs. Morley gave Marion a disapproving look.

"Okay, how's this?"

"Better, still not quite right. Hold on, just had a brainstorm."

Marion reached into her purse and pulled out a heavy revolver.

"What are you doing? What is that?"

"A 1917 Colt .45, military issue, from World War I."

"Where did you get that?"

"My desk drawer."

"You have a pistol in your desk drawer?"

"Doesn't everyone?"

"No?"

Marion laughed. "Clara, hold this up for the picture, it's not loaded, checked three times." She handed the revolver to Clara.

She raised her phone again. "Not quite, almost there." She stepped out of the room, returning a moment later with a metal detector.

Simon's eyes narrowed. "Where did you get that? Did you plan all this?"

"Of course not, I saw it sitting in the atrium when I came in. It will add a little *je ne sais quois* to the photo, help you remember this momentous day when you're old and gray. Memories, am I right? So important to hold on to them, cherish them forever."

Simon looked at the revolver Clara was holding, then back to Marion. "You're up to something, I know you are."

"So young and so suspicious. Heartbreaking is what it is. Sad."

"Totally up to something." Simon took the metal detector, holding it in front of him. "Go ahead, take your picture."

Marion raised her phone. "Look happy, you just solved four cold case murders. Now look serious, you just solved four cold case murders. Not that serious, it's not a funeral. Now look at each other. No, look into each other's eyes, act like lovebirds. Now look scared, like you're creeping around down in the basement and you just saw a ghost."

Five minutes later Marion lowered her phone. "That should do it, there's a good one in there somewhere. Great photos, I'll send you a print, suitable for framing. I should charge you. But I won't."

Sergeant Rogers was getting up just as a very anxious Mrs. Morley stepped into the room, setting a silver tray of cookies on the coffee table.

"Did anyone else hear that rattling noise coming from the basement?"

# Chapter 26

Simon and Clara were in the old pickup truck, the windows open, wind whistling through the cab as they drove.

"What do you think Bobby will say when we tell him about Josiah being framed by Chief Merrick?"

"I don't know, but I'm glad we're doing it before the article hits the paper."

"Do you think our names will be in the paper?"

"Sergeant Rogers said they might be, but not a single word about ghosts. We were just a couple of teenagers who found a skeleton in their basement and began our own investigation."

"Does he think we talk to ghosts?"

"He doesn't want to know, as long as there's hard evidence to back up our story."

"A lot of people are like that, I guess. Scared of ghosts."

"People are afraid of things they don't understand.

Simon glanced over at Clara, taking her hand, just in time to see her scream. "Stop! Look out!"

Simon slammed on the brakes, the tires squealing. "What is it?"

Clara pointed to the soldier standing in the road ahead of them.

"It's him again. Who is that guy? What does he want?"

The man in the brown military uniform stood at attention, the butt of his rifle resting on the pavement, his eyes on Simon and Clara. Once again he gave a sharp salute, holding it for three seconds, then faded away.

Clara said, "This is so strange, who is he?"

"I told you, it's a classic case of saluting ghost syndrome."

"That's not a thing and you know it."

"It could be, stranger things have happened."

Ten minutes later they were in the general store parking lot, heading for the front door.

Simon pulled the door open, waving to Bobby Finch as they stepped inside.

Bobby said, "Let me guess, you're here to borrow my new metal detector?" He laughed.

"No, it's something else, something about your grandfather, Josiah Finch."

"What about him?"

"This is going to take a while, we should sit down."

"We can sit in the lunch room."

It took half an hour to tell Bobby everything they had discovered about the murder of Josiah Finch, how he had been framed by Chief Merrick.

Bobby rubbed his chin. "Don't take this the wrong way, but we always knew he was innocent."

"How did you know?"

"I guess I can tell you now. Josiah drank because of what happened to him in the war."

"What happened?"

"He was in the Battle of Belleau Wood in 1918. It was a major battle near the end of World War I, during the German spring offensive near the Marne River in France. There were over ten thousand casualties, almost two thousand soldiers died. They said Josiah had shell shock when he came home; that's what they called it back then. Now we call it PTSD. Back then they just expected you to come home and forget about everything you saw, get on with your life. Except it doesn't work that way. My dad said Josiah had nightmares for years, he would wake up screaming, reliving the war in his dreams. It scared my grandma about to death when it happened. Scared my dad too."

"That's why Josiah drank? Because of the war?"

"It was the only way he could sleep, and it got worse after my grandma passed. He wouldn't live with us, moved into that little house in the forest, wanted to be alone."

"That's awful."

"The thing is, he hated guns after the war, didn't want anything to do with them. He didn't own a gun, so there's no way he would have taken his own life with one, or shot someone. My dad told the police that at the time, but they didn't care, they said the police chief saw him do it."

"Merrick was lying."

"Of course he was, but everyone believed him because he was the police chief."

"There's going to be a story in the paper about it. You should tell them what you just told us, it's important for people to know about Josiah. I can call the paper, have them talk to you."

"I'd like that, to finally clear his name. I have something to show you, wait here." He left the room, returning a few minutes later with an envelope and a velvet box.

"What is that?"

"Josiah's medals from the war." He opened the box, sliding it across the table to Simon and Clara. "He got a Silver Star and the Distinguished Service Medal for his actions in the Battle of Belleau Wood. We know he lost a lot of friends there, but he never talked about the war, what happened there."

"I'm sorry."

"I have a photograph of him, maybe the paper could put it in the article."

"I know they would."

Bobby opened the envelope, sliding out an old sepia tone image of a young man with a bright smile wearing a World War I uniform. He turned it around, sliding it over to them. "That's Josiah, it was taken a few days before he shipped off to the war in Europe."

Simon froze when he saw it. The soldier who had saluted them on the highway was Josiah Finch.

\* \* \* \* \*

Simon strolled into the kitchen, spotting Mrs. Morley seated at the table, deeply engrossed in the morning paper. This was odd, it was 7:30 and she hadn't started breakfast yet.

"Mrs. Morley, are you okay?"

She lowered the newspaper, looked at him, then raised it again.

"What's wrong? Did something happen?"

Mrs. Morley turned the paper around, silently holding it up for Simon to read the large bold-faced headline running across the front page.

## Caligo Falls Teens Solve
## Four Cold Case Murders!

Simon stared blankly at the large photo of him and Clara, pistol and metal detector in hand. He let out a screech. "How did they get that photo?"

Mrs. Morley pointed to the tiny print underneath the photo.

*Photo courtesy of Marion Jaggers*

"I knew it! I knew she was up to something!"

Simon pulled out a chair, sitting down next to Mrs. Morley, both of them reading the article.

His phone beeped, a text from Clara.

*DID YOU SEE THE PAPER????*

*Reading it now. I don't believe this. Marion tricked us, took that crazy photo. It was for the newspaper!*

*It's a good photo of us though. You look really handsome.*

*Really?*

*Really.*

318

*You look beautiful, even with that pistol.*

*Thanks. Don't worry, we won't be famous in college, just in Caligo Falls.*

*The only thing that matters is we cleared Josiah's name. There's a lot in the article about him and what happened in World War I at the battle of Belleau Wood, and his PTSD.*

*You're right, it's not just about us.*

*See you tomorrow!*

*Can't wait!*

\* \* \* \* \*

"You're sure you don't want me to go with you?"

"I'm sure, I have everything I need, GPS is all programmed. My roommate is from Cambridge, he's going to meet us there and show us around. He sounds really nice. Harvard is only a short bus ride from MIT."

"Clara, you have everything you need?"

Clara's mom laughed. "More than everything she'll

need."

Kate put her hand on Simon's shoulder. "You'll drive safely?"

"Yes, my plan is to drive super fast so I'll spend less time on the road, which equates to less time available for possible car accidents."

Clara punched his arm. "Don't be an idiot."

Marion Jaggers let out a loud squawk. "Lovebirds!" She clapped Simon on the back. "Well done, kiddos! Bobby is ecstatic about clearing his grandfather's name, can't stop talking about it. I might have to buy some earplugs. He's even talking about writing a book, *Murders in Caligo Falls,* the story of how his grandfather was framed for the murder of Frederick Thornton. Who doesn't love stories about murders and corrupt rich guys? He'll probably make a million." She handed a paper bag to Simon. "Just in case you miss me."

Simon peered into the bag, grinning. "Oreo cookies, thanks!"

"I expect to see both of you at the art exhibition in October, no excuses. Everyone wants to meet Edmund's great nephew and Emma Weatherby's granddaughter."

"We'll be there, I promise. I can't wait to see the haunted painting."

Mrs. Morley frowned. "Who would ever want to see a haunted painting?" She handed a pink cardboard box to Simon. "A chocolate cake, just in case you get hungry on the drive to Boston."

"Yum, thanks Mrs. Morley. That was so nice of you."

Harrington stepped forward, a small package in hand, wrapped in brown paper, securely tied with coarse green twine. "A little gift for you and Clara, courtesy of Edmund Wilder."

"What is it?"

"I have not even a glimmer of an idea what it might possibly be."

Clara laughed.

Simon took the package, slipping it into his backpack, setting it behind the front seat of the truck. He finished strapping down the boxes and suitcases in the bed of the truck, saying, "I guess that's it, we're good to go. All secure."

Kate gave Simon and Clara long hugs. "You be careful and study hard. No wild parties. Well, maybe one or two, but not too wild. Call us if you need anything at all."

"I will."

After many hugs and fond farewells, Simon and Clara climbed into the truck, the newly serviced V-8 engine smoothly roaring to life. Simon put the truck in gear, Clara turning around and waving as they headed down the gravel drive.

They were halfway to the main road when Clara gave

a shout.

"Stop!"

"What is it? Did you forget something?"

"Put the ghost ring on."

"Why?"

"Just do it. I have a feeling."

Simon slipped the ring on, taking Clara's hand. They turned around, looking through the rear window, their eyes on a man in a dapper white suit and hat, a lovely woman wearing a long red dress standing next to him. The woman in the red dress waved to them, the man smiled.

"I knew they were here. I just knew it. They came to say goodbye."

Simon and Clara waved farewell to Edmund Wilder and Emma Weatherby, watching until they both faded away and were gone.

Clara slid over next to Simon. "Did I mention my dorm is supposed to be haunted?"

If you enjoyed reading

*The Ghost Ring* • *Shadows of Caligo Falls*

please leave a short review or rating
on Amazon.com
Reviews are the lifeblood of indie publishers –
we can't survive without them!

If you have any comments or suggestions
or would like to be notified of upcoming book
releases and Free Kindle book day promotions,
please email me at
*OrvilleMouse@gmail.com*

Follow me at:
*www.facebook.com/TomHoffmanAuthor/*


Best wishes until we meet again,

*Tom Hoffman*

# ABOUT THE AUTHOR

Tom Hoffman received a B.S. in psychology
from Georgetown University
and a B.A. from the now-defunct
Oregon College of Art. He has lived in Alaska
with his wife since 1973. They have two
adult children and three adorable
grandchildren. Tom was a graphic designer
and artist for over 35 years.
Redirecting his imagination from art to
writing, he wrote his first novel,
The Eleventh Ring, at age 63